A UNITED SHIFTER FORCE CHRISTMAS

TERRY SPEAR

Wilde Ink Publishing

A United Shifter Force Christmas

Previously published as part of the Shifters and Mistletoe Anthology.

Copyright © 2021 by Terry Spear

Cover Copyright by Terry Spear

Discover more about Terry Spear at:

http://www.terryspear.com/

Print ISBN: 978-1-63311-083-0

Ebook ISBN: 978-1-63311-082-3

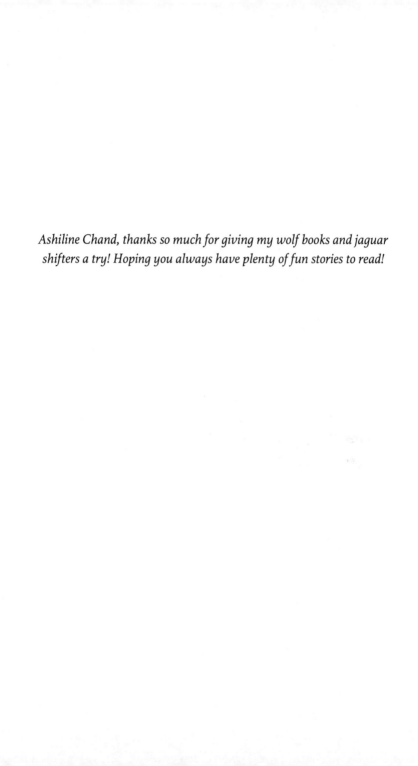

Ashiline Chand, thanks so much for giving my wolf books and jaguar shifters a try! Hoping you always have plenty of fun stories to read!

SYNOPSIS

Rowdy Sanderson, a special agent for the United Shifter Force, a group of jaguars and wolves who aid shifters in trouble and deal with those who *are* trouble, isn't even one of them. But he wants to be a wolf in the worst way. When a special agent needs help at her USF branch in Ely, Minnesota, he volunteers because he's the only one in Houston without a family for the holidays. Maybe he will still get his Christmas wish—to be a wolf shifter like some of his friends and coworkers so he will have their "superpowers" to do his job.

Justine Winters is grateful the director of the USF is sending a special agent to her branch in Ely to aid her if she gets swamped. He's really hot, according to the photos the director sent her of Rowdy, but is he a wolf or a jaguar? Preferably a wolf. But then she learns he's human! No one's supposed to know that shifters exist. No way will he be able to sniff out shifters and assist her. She reluctantly agrees to accept him—figuring she'll have to put him on desk duty.

All that changes when she meets the real man—who desperately wants to be a wolf, who grows on her just like the director said he would, who risks his life for shifters, who she defends to others of her kind for working with the USF. But being the one to bite him has consequences and nothing's turning out the way she planned.

1

——————

"As you know, we started a United Shifter Force (USF) branch in Ely, Minnesota," Martin Sullivan said to the gathered wolves and jaguars of the branch in Houston, Texas. The jaguar shifter was the director of the special elite force of the jaguar shifter force known as the JAG or Golden Claw. When they began having issues with wolves and jaguars working together in criminal pursuits, he formed the United Shifter Force and was also the director over that.

"We need to loan out one of our special agents from this location to assist the lone agent up there until we can hire someone more permanent. I thought we would be able to hire an agent before this, but I haven't had any luck, especially during the holidays. The jaguars with our organization prefer to stay more in the south. The wolves and jaguars have family here and have plans to spend Christmas with them," Martin said.

Rowdy Sanderson figured something like this might happen when Martin couldn't hire another shifter to help the agent out, and he raised his hand. "I volunteer." He was the only human who worked for the organization, and he had no family to spend the holidays with.

Formerly a homicide detective, he was from Bigfork, Montana, when, during his investigations, he learned both wolf and jaguar shifters existed. Normally, someone would have turned or eliminated him, but for helping them solve a case, they allowed him to join the organization.

For the winter, he would love working in the north instead of Texas. With volunteering to go to Minnesota, he was looking forward to seeing some snow.

One of the jaguar families had invited him to join them for Christmas Eve dinner, and one of the wolf families wanted him to have Christmas dinner with them. They truly were like one big shifter family—despite his being a human in a mix of shifters.

Otherwise, he was free to help another agent in the USF who needed his assistance.

"All right. Thanks, Rowdy. You're always great for stepping in to help us out," Martin said, looking vastly relieved that he didn't have to "volunteer" someone else for the assignment.

Rowdy didn't mind, though he thoroughly enjoyed working with the shifters here and they understood his desire to be one of them, body and soul. A wolf though, not a jaguar. He thought he would blend in better as a wolf in most places, and he just had an affinity for the wolves, more so than with the jaguars. He had solid friendships with the jaguars too, but he wanted to be a wolf versus a big cat. Though he had to remind himself the jaguars had no shifting issues with the full moon phase like newly turned wolves did. And he could still shift during the new moon, unlike with new wolves.

Still, working with someone up north who had no knowledge of his situation as far as him being human could be a problem. The shifters used their heightened senses of smell and hearing and night vision to work on their cases, all of which he was sorely lacking. Their missions were to help shifters in need of assistance and incarcerate or eliminate those—depending on the severity of the situation—who were causing trouble.

He felt he had to stay in their good graces because their motto was to turn someone who knew what they were or eliminate him. None of the *lupus garou* wanted to turn Rowdy and have to babysit him when he would have shifting issues during the full moon phase. And nobody wanted to terminate him because he really was good at his job.

"When did you need me up there?"

"Yesterday."

Rowdy smiled. "Yes, sir. Merry Christmas, everyone. I'll see you when I return."

The women gave him hugs and well wishes. The guys slapped him on the back and shook his hand. He knew they were glad *he* was the one who was going and not any of *them*. He figured this was the best Christmas gift he could give his coworkers that really meant something to them.

He just hoped the guy he was going to be working with in Ely wouldn't want to terminate him when he arrived!

SPECIAL AGENT JUSTINE Winters was thrilled Martin Sullivan was loaning her one of his agents located at the USF branch in Houston to assist her on the job at her branch in Ely, Minnesota until the director could hire someone suitable for a permanent position where she was located.

"I'll call you back as soon as I know who I'll be sending." Martin hadn't had any success so far in hiring someone and she hoped that the guy he was sending would be amenable to hanging around for a while if it took some time—though she really needed to wait to see if she and he were even compatible to be thinking such a thing.

As a gray wolf, she'd been excited to open the Ely branch, having been a former police detective in Minneapolis, civilian police department, of course. When she learned jaguar shifters were attempting to open a United Shifter Force branch in other areas, she jumped at the chance to leave the city and move to Ely where here parents still lived.

She'd already had to track down two teen bear shifters who had raided farmers' beehives back in September. She'd thought they'd been regular bears, but she'd smelled their deodorant and shampoo when she'd investigated. Once she'd caught them red handed—well, pawed—while raiding yet another farmer's beehive, she had turned them over to their bear sleuth leader to deal with them.

An Arctic wolf pack lived in the area too, some working as private investigators, who had kindly offered to do any investigations she needed as a courtesy to her since she was a wolf too—though a gray—and on her own.

Martin called her back. "Okay, I've got confirmation that Rowdy Sanderson will be heading up your way shortly. He's gone home to pack. He's a former homicide detective with the Bigfork, Montana police department and began working with the USF shortly after it was formed." Martin sent her some pictures of Rowdy.

Her jaw dropped. He was drop-dead sexy, muscled, dark eyes that were alight with mischief, dark hair like hers, and he wore a trim beard—in a word, gorgeous. If she had any trouble with unruly shifters, she was siccing Rowdy on them. Muscles on top of muscles, he looked like he could handle any trouble that came his way. Though he wore a hint of a smile that was at once charming and disarming at the same time.

He was probably mated. Or a *jaguar* shifter.

She frowned at the rest of the pictures Martin sent to her of Rowdy where he appeared to be in the middle of survival training, shirtless in every one of them, showing off all those spectacular muscles, glistening with sweat in the sun.

"How come you don't have any of him with his shirt on?" she asked, before she could stop herself. Not that she minded eyeing the veritable hunk sans shirt, but she just thought it odd that the director wouldn't be sending her an official photo of him—fully dressed.

"I couldn't find his official USF photo, just the ones of him that were taken while he was in training when he had his shirt off. I suspect one of our she-cats took the pictures and uploaded them in his personal file to tease her mate. Maybe a couple of the female shifters did it. They all really like him and he's good-natured about their teasing."

If they'd been humans in a human organization, they could have been in trouble for sexual harassment. But as shifters, they didn't see it that way.

Justine chuckled. She wished, in a way, that she worked with them in the same branch since she'd heard they really enjoyed working with each other, but she loved the cold winters here. She couldn't imagine feeling the Christmas spirit in hot Texas. Besides, she'd finally gotten a job close to home, so she was staying here.

Then she realized Rowdy had to be unmated, or the mated women wouldn't be showing off his abs. She smiled. Hmm, maybe Justine could convince him to stay here permanently and work with her. If she liked him.

"One other thing."

She didn't like the ominous tone of Martin's voice. Now she suspected he was sending her trouble. Maybe Rowdy lived up to his name and didn't get along with the agents at the Houston branch and that's why he volunteered to come up here. But was he a wolf? Or a jaguar?

"Rowdy is human."

"What?" She had every reason to be shocked at the news. Humans didn't work for the USF! She couldn't imagine having a human working for them and they would have to hide what they were or what they were looking for—shifters in trouble or causing trouble.

"He knows about us. About wolves and jaguars and he's an excellent agent."

If Martin thought he was such a great agent, why was he foisting Rowdy off on her?

"Just work with him. You'll see."

"He can't even identify a shifter from a human. And if I have to track down a shifter and interrogate him or her, the shifter perp probably won't want to confess anything in front of a human and fear giving away our secrets." She thought Rowdy could be a real liability.

"It's your branch. You do what you want with him. Give him desk duty. We did for the first six months he worked for us for the same reason you're probably reluctant to work with him. But he truly is damn good at his job, and he'll be a real asset if you give him half a chance."

Here, after seeing the pictures of the half-naked hunk, she was looking forward to taking Rowdy home to show him off to her family even. If he had been a wolf.

But he wasn't even a shifter? What a waste of such a beautiful body.

"All right? He's on his way, eager to help, but he'll understand if you don't feel you can trust him right away and sideline him for a while."

"Why are you sending him and not a wolf? Or a jaguar?" She had to keep reminding herself they were a *united* shifter force of the two and that even Martin was a jaguar himself and had hired her.

"All the other agents are married and it's getting so close to

Christmas that they're spending the holidays with family. Rowdy doesn't have any family."

Now she felt like a real heel.

"I needed someone to volunteer. We don't know how long it will take before we can hire another shifter to work with you. So in the meantime, Rowdy volunteered. We can always swap him out with someone else after the holidays."

Justine chewed on her bottom lip. "All right." She should be grateful Martin was sending her anyone to work with her this close to the holidays. Rowdy could answer the phones and do investigations from the office.

"What cases do you have right now?" Martin asked.

Martin didn't normally ask her about her caseload though it was important to know how busy she was really going to be to justify having another body working in the office. "I had a case of some people stealing Christmas trees, but when I looked into it, they were human, and I turned them over to the police. I've got to meet with the bear sleuth leader over the issue of the teens breaking into beehives in September and see how they're doing. I've had a lot of random cases that have been keeping me busy but not overwhelmed."

"Okay, good. So you're really not swamped with cases right now."

"No. Just a few minor incidents have arisen, but I'm managing. At least for this week." But she and Martin knew that what was fine right now could turn into a disaster if she didn't have help and she got a couple of bad cases. Like she had last week. But she couldn't quit thinking about Rowdy and how he knew about the shifters, and he hadn't been turned or terminated. "So about Rowdy, is he afraid one of you might turn him?"

"No. He wants to be a wolf and have superpowers."

"Superpowers."

"Yeah. Our increased longevity, quicker healing abilities, and

how effective our senses are compared to humans. He feels he
would be much more of an asset if he was a shifter like us. But
he prefers to be a wolf. Of course it all depends on if a wolf is
willing to turn him."

"Well, if you, or he, have any notion I'm going to turn him,
you both can forget it."

"I'm just sending him up there to help if you need it. He'll
have lodging at one of the hotels that the USF will pay for, or he
might stay at a wolf-run cabin, his choice."

"Thanks. I'm grateful, truly."

"You'll like Rowdy. Even though he's a human, he grows on
everyone. I'll check in with you later, or if you really don't suit,
just send him back to us." Martin didn't say he'd send anyone
else to replace him, she noted.

"Right." No way would she send him packing. She'd put him
to work and make do somehow just in case the workload picked
up and she *was* swamped.

Two days later, Rowdy arrived in Ely at White Birch Resort on the north shore of Birch Lake, everything covered in about a half a foot of snow. Several of the trees, all the cabins, the main house, and the lodge were decorated in Christmas lights at the wolf-run resort. It really was cheery to see it after the long drive up here. He figured he'd enjoy the lake at night after he finished work, if he was off. In this business, he never knew what the situation would entail. He wished he was a shifter so he could take care of cases on his own. Instead, he was dependent on the shifters to tell him who was one and who required assistance or who needed to be taken into custody and charged with a crime.

He dropped his bags on the cabin's wood floor and saw a Christmas tree decorated in wolves and bows in the living room. He smiled, then called the USF office here to talk to the agent running the branch. "Hi, this is Rowdy Sanderson, ready to report for duty."

"Justine Winters, your temporary boss. You must have driven hours and hours yesterday to get in by lunch today." She sounded surprised.

"I did, but I wanted to be here if you needed me. No sense in prolonging the journey."

"You're not a workaholic, are you?"

"A bit of one."

"Okay, well, if you haven't had lunch, eat, and then join me at the office." She gave him the address, though Martin had already given it to him.

"Thanks. I'll run to the store and get some things to stock the kitchen and be at the office in a little while."

"All right. No rush. I'm going to have some lunch at home, and I'll see you when you get to the office."

"See you then." Rowdy ended the call and headed to the store. He had been trying to get a read on Justine while having the brief conversation with her. Martin must have told her he was human. From the tone of her voice on the phone, she seemed all right with it. Not overwhelmingly welcoming, but he figured he would have to prove to her he could do the job, just as he had done with the others he had worked with. It didn't sound like she had anything pressing to take care of and that was good while he got settled in. Though he was always ready to work on a mission at a moment's notice.

At the grocery store, he grabbed several items to set up housekeeping, a couple of choice steaks, and a microwave lasagna to make for lunch, then returned to the cabin. He loved the cabin and setting. From the back windows, he could see the lake, and though he felt it was too cold to sit out to eat—he needed to become acclimated to the colder winter up here—he could enjoy the vista from the living room.

He put away all the groceries and then he started heating the lasagna in the microwave. At the branch in Houston, he worked extra-long hours on the job, well, mainly because he didn't have anything else to do. No hobbies. His lifelong pursuit, besides catching killers and putting them behind bars, had been to prove to himself that shifters existed. Now?

He needed a mate. And nobody needed him. For a whole six months, they wouldn't let him go on actual missions with the other special agents in the branch. He had been a desk jockey, and he had wished they had trusted him earlier to get the missions done. Though he understood that it was hard to imagine he could get the right bad guy when he couldn't smell that they were even shifters. But he still liked working with the agents. It had given him a whole new meaning to his life. He hoped Justine didn't stick him with desk duty here.

He didn't even want to date humans now. He had to wait for the right shifter to come along who would fall in love with him and want to turn him.

The microwaved dinged and he pulled out his lasagna just as he got a call from Justine.

"What's up?" Rowdy asked, getting ready to move his lasagna from the microwave box to a plate. Everyone back at the office always gave him a hard time when he made a microwave meal at work because he had to clean a dish then. To his way of thinking, a meal was something to be enjoyed, even if he didn't cook it from scratch. Eating it on a real plate made it seem more home-cooked, not so rushed.

"I need your help immediately. Come to my place." Justine gave him the address, sounding like she was breathless, running. "Go to the rear of the house. Two teens have fallen through the ice on the lake. They're bear shifters, two I've dealt with before."

He shoved his lasagna into the fridge and was in the Land Rover in a jiffy. "Have you called emergency services?"

"One's in his bear suit. I've called both the bear sleuth leader and the teen's father, but they're located a lot farther out than you are."

"I'm already halfway there." The adrenaline was pumping through his blood at an accelerated rate, readying him to do whatever was necessary to save the teens. He was glad she still had the phone line open to him. "Did both boys go into the water?"

"Yes! I'm almost to them."

"Be careful. Do you have ropes? Blankets?"

"Yes!"

"I'll be there in another few minutes."

KENNY AND ANDREW BRIXWORTH were a handful. Justine couldn't believe they'd be in trouble again. This was nothing like the beehive incident though. This was a much more deadly venture. Still, if a beehive farmer had shot at the teens while raiding his beehives, that could have been another story.

At a run, she dropped the two blankets and her phone on the snow some distance from where the ice was cracking, and the white pickup truck was sinking. With a rope in hand, she inched out the rest of the way toward the boys and the expanding cracks in the ice. The teens had driven the medium-sized truck across the frozen lake. Fishing poles were sitting on the ice nearby to fish, it appeared. The trouble wasn't so much from driving on the ice—they'd made it a long way out—but that they'd parked it in place—and the constant load had caused the ice to give. They'd needed twelve to fifteen inches of blue ice to drive that heavy of a vehicle out there. Obviously, it wasn't thick enough.

When she'd heard their yells while she was getting ready to have lunch, she'd peered out the window and seen them, the truck sinking into the lake, the boy and the bear trying to get out of the water. At least they'd been outside of the truck.

She was getting closer to them when she heard a Land Rover's car door slam in front of her house, and she hoped help was on its way.

"Justine!" Rowdy called out.

"Here!" She looked back to see Rowdy wearing a parka and boots, cargo pants, no hat, and he was racing across the ice until he could reach where she was trying to get to the boys. "It's cracking all over the place. Be careful."

"I've rescued ice fishermen before," he said, taking the rope from her and moving faster than she thought was safe.

If they all ended up in the water, they'd be doomed.

Rowdy pulled off his parka, and she envisioned him stripping down to his waist like he'd been in his photos. Instead, he tied the rope to himself and tossed the end to Kenny, who was in his human form. Andrew was trying to push him up from where he was beside him in the water using his bear's strength, but he couldn't manage.

"Grab hold and I'll pull you out," Rowdy said to Kenny.

The truck was nearly out of sight now, and despite worrying about the boys, she had the fleeting thought that their dad was not going to be happy that they'd lost the truck to an icy grave.

But Kenny's hands were too cold, and he couldn't keep a grip on the rope as Rowdy tried to ease him out.

"Okay, just hold on. I'm coming to you." When Rowdy reached Kenny, he wrapped the rope underneath his arms and knotted it, then he pulled him slowly out of the water, the ice cracking more, the ominous sound making Justine cringe as she drew closer.

"Can you take him to the shore and wrap him in a blanket?" Rowdy asked.

"I'm not sure he can make it on his own power." She figured he'd have to be carried.

Rowdy went to help Andrew, but he climbed out of the water

as a bear, having more strength and his fur coat had helped to keep him warm. But as soon as he got out of the lake water, the ice cracked even more, and they were all scrambling to get away from the threat before they all ended up in the frigid water. She realized then that Andrew had stayed in the water as a bear to try and save his brother.

Rowdy grabbed Kenny up in his arms and hollered, "Come on!"

Justine seized Rowdy's coat and this time they all ran, though she wanted to tell Andrew to spread out further from them as his heavier, lumbering gait was causing the ice to crack even more. And they needed to move away from each other to disperse the weight. But he wanted to stick close to them as if he knew that his salvation was in staying with them. She ran as fast she could to safety so that at least she wasn't adding to the weight on the ice.

She heard a vehicle park out front of her house and saw two men, the boys' father, Simon, and their uncle, Benton, running to help them. Then she heard another two vehicles park at her place and more men ran to assist them. She reached the blankets on the shore and Rowdy came in right behind her and they wrapped Kenny in the blankets.

"We can take him in the house and warm him up," Justine said.

"He can shift once he gets out of his wet clothes in your house." Simon glanced at Andrew, who hung his bear head low.

Then the uncle untied the rope attached to Kenny and the dad lifted him in his arms and carried him to the house. Rowdy's own shirt was sopping wet, and he had to be freezing too.

Rowdy untied the rope to himself, and she hurried everyone inside her house to warm up the boys and Rowdy.

"Do you have extra clothes for the boys?" she asked the dad.

"Yeah, I do." Simon headed outside to his truck.

She wrapped Kenny in more warm blankets and brought Andrew and Kenny some towels for when they changed into dry clothes.

When the dad came back in, he helped his son strip and dress because he was still so cold, his fingers were numb, and he was shivering hard. "You change too, Andrew."

Justine went to get Rowdy a spare shirt—an oversized one that she slept in, just a blue and red, flannel plaid shirt, nothing girly. She hoped he wouldn't mind that she'd worn it last night. But it was the biggest shirt she had, and it was nice and warm.

He smiled at her and thanked her.

Everyone else was getting Kenny warmed up and Andrew had shifted and changed into the spare clothes.

She couldn't help but watch Rowdy remove his sopping wet shirt, baring his in-the-flesh, wet abs—realizing she should have brought him a towel and shouldn't be eyeing him as her next meal. She finally said, "Let me get you a towel too." She was ready to dry him off personally, as *if* he needed her help. She returned with a towel for Rowdy.

"Is Kenny going to be all right?" she asked, tearing her gaze from Rowdy wiping down his beautiful chest.

"Yeah. We'll take it from here. You might have to hire another agent just for—" The dad stopped speaking and frowned at Rowdy.

"He's a special agent working with me." Working *for* me, she meant to say. She didn't bother explaining why a human would be working for the USF branch.

"We'll get out of your hair so you can take care of real business." The dad looked like he was glad the boys were safe but irritated to the max that they could have lost their lives, put others in danger, and lost the truck.

"Sorry, Dad," Andrew said.

"Yeah, sorry." Kenny and his brother looked like they were in really hot water.

Then they all left along with the other men, whom she hadn't met, all bear shifters. She caught Rowdy taking a whiff of her shirt. Yeah, it smelled like peaches and cream—the body-wash she'd used last night before she put the shirt on, but she didn't expect him to smell it.

He smiled a little in that sexy, too charming way she'd seen in his photos, and then he pulled on the shirt.

She sighed as he buttoned a few of the buttons and left the top few undone.

"Thanks for saving Kenny. I would never have been able to get him out of the water in time," she said.

"He had no strength in his upper arms after being in the water for so long. I'm just glad they survived. I thought maybe the other boy in his bear coat had been injured when he didn't get out of the water, then realized he was trying to push his brother out of the lake, but he just couldn't manage. At least his bear fur had kept him warm enough."

"Right. The boys seem really close to each other and it's heartwarming to see them stick together like that." She glanced at the slow cooker. "Did...did you manage to eat anything for lunch?"

"Uh, no. I heated up a microwave container of lasagna, got your distress call, and put it back in the fridge."

"Would you like some hot chili and something hot to drink for lunch then? I made the chili this morning to have this afternoon." She figured he needed something hot after being doused with so much of that icy water, carrying a soaking wet Kenny, and wearing no coat.

"Yeah, sure, it smells great, if it won't put you out too much."

"Are you kidding? After you earned your pay and then some today?"

"I'm glad I could be there for you and for them. What can I do to help?"

"You can set the table, if you don't mind." She pointed to the silverware drawer and then dished up the hot chili from the slow cooker.

"I was just lucky that Andrew could make it out of the lake on his own power. I wasn't sure I could lift the bear."

"Yeah, I don't think either of us could have managed that feat, though he's not a full-grown bear. He's still hefty as a bear. Did you want a sprinkle of cheddar cheese on your chili?"

"That would be great."

She sprinkled shredded cheese on both their bowls of hot chili. "Coffee?"

"Sure, thanks." Then he took the bowls to the table.

She brought over a tray of coffee cups, a bowl of sugar, and the creamer, placed them on the table, and sat across from him, the dining room open to the living room.

She was glad the Christmas tree was all lit up, sitting next to the big picture window, presents under the tree all wrapped in gold and decorated with gold ribbons. Warm honey-oak wood bookcases were built into one wall, brown velour wrap-around seating took center stage, and a big screen TV was prominently featured on another wall. Everything felt warm and welcoming while outside it was snowy and cold.

"So tell me how you came to know about us and began working for the USF." Justine had thought about it for the two days it took Rowdy to drive up to Ely. She never believed he would hotfoot it up here that quickly, just so he could be there if she needed him, and boy, did she now. She really appreciated him for it. No way was she giving him desk duty.

She just couldn't imagine how he would have learned about shifters, though, and no one had done anything about it— except hired him to work with a shifter force!

"Martin probably told you I was a homicide detective working out of Bigfork, Montana. A gray wolf shifter pack lives on the lake if you didn't know that. They were having trouble with another shifter pack, and I was called in to investigate some wolf-chewed up, naked dead guys."

"Easy to arouse some suspicion if you already were thinking of a paranormal twist to the homicides."

"Exactly. Then later I began checking out a situation with Arctic wolves that had purportedly saved some sledders who had caused an avalanche and been buried alive in Minnesota. I was in the area at the time seeing a friend and naturally I had to check it out."

"Naturally. Martin said you knew about jaguars too."

"Well, the Arctic wolves ended up going to Houston and started investigating a case I was looking into. Long story short, I learned jaguars were shifters also. And when they were having trouble with wolves and jaguars, the United Shifter Force was formed. Since I had helped them with the case involving both jaguars and wolves, they went ahead and hired me to work full time. I mean, the shifters had a choice once they knew what I knew—turn me or eliminate me. But I'm really good at my job and have a high success rate of finding and putting away murderers, so they agreed to take me into the organization that was created and funded by jaguars. Just in case you're interested in knowing, I want to be a wolf, not a jaguar shifter, if I have a choice. My friends in the USF tell me often enough that it might not be my choice. Except for those who know me, I have to keep mum with shifters outside of the office about me knowing anything concerning the shifter kind. Not everyone is completely understanding about it. I wasn't even sure how you would feel."

"Shocked." She wasn't going to lie about it. She finished her bowl of chili and was considering having a little more when she got a call from David Davis, an Arctic wolf, private investigator with a group here, all more newly turned.

"We need your USF help," David said, and from the sounds of it, he was out in the woods somewhere hiking.

Now what?

3

"We're on our way." Justine ended the call and said to Rowdy, "I got a message from a local Arctic wolf shifter, David Davis, who got an anonymous call from a man who said two wolves were injured in the woods near here. In case it was just a hoax, he and his partner, Cameron, went out to investigate and found two injured males, in their thirties, gray wolf shifters, and get this—the telltale bite marks were that of a jaguar. Which is why we have picked up the case."

Rowdy thought Justine sounded like she was accepting him on the team, and he was relieved. "Had the men been wearing their wolf coats?"

He studied Justine, a beautiful brunette with pretty green eyes, and she seemed to see everything. She was wearing a soft fuzzy red sweater and white parka and looked perfectly huggable. Black slacks and black boots finished the ensemble.

"Yeah. There are patches of gray wolf fur all over, indicating they had put up a real fight. They were still in their wolf forms when David found them, so at least their wolf coats were protecting them from the elements."

"So no ID."

"No, not that David or Cameron found. The men are private investigators, so this has become a USF investigation."

"Cameron? David Davis? I know of them. I haven't met them personally, but I know their partner, Owen Nottingham and his mate, Candice. They're the ones that saved the sledders involved in the avalanche. What did the wolves say?"

"They're badly injured and not talking. David and Cameron picked them up and took them to a doctor who's a *lupus garou*. You and I need to check out the crime scene. The PIs didn't want to mess it up any more than they might have by coming across the men and moving them. But they're former police officers out of Seattle, Washington so they know how to preserve a crime scene. Though in this case—now that they're all shifters—things have to be done differently."

Like hiding bodies from the local police if they were killed by a shifter in their fur coat.

"We need to search for the men's clothes. And then see if we can run across any scent trails to pinpoint where the jaguar took off to. Most of us don't leave any ID in our clothes when we shift to run in our wilder forms. We don't want anyone to know who we are if someone runs across them and believes something bad has happened to the person wearing them," she said.

"Gotcha." Though Rowdy already knew this, he figured she might not realize how much he did know about their shifter world.

She put the remaining chili in the fridge, and Rowdy hurried to put the dishes in the dishwasher.

Then they grabbed up their parkas and headed out to her car.

"The Arctic wolves didn't recognize either of the gray wolves," she said.

If it hadn't been so close to Christmas, Rowdy would have

thought this was Halloween as they drove to the crime scene. They had more crazy cases like this than at any other time of year.

She parked off the road where the crime had been committed and they both got out to begin to search for any clues.

He did notice jaguar paw prints leading to and from the area. "We need to cast the prints."

"Yes, I'm photographing them. The plaster is in my car. We want to clear the scene as soon as possible," Justine said. "We sure don't want anyone other than our kind learning of it."

He suspected she realized her mistake in saying "our" kind, since he wasn't one of their kind. "Yeah, I agree." He was so used to working normal dead body scenes, until he began working for USF, that it took some getting used to how the protocols were so different.

He retrieved the plaster and mixed it to the consistency of half-melted ice cream. Then he poured it into the track. Once he was finished and it had solidified, he put it in her vehicle.

They kept crimes like this secret from the regular police as much as possible. No reporters. They had to take any evidence and the injured shifters or the bodies away. If the shifters had died, they had to examine them in their own doctor's office. They had to pretend none of this existed because they couldn't have human law enforcement searching for a shifter murderer or other shifter criminals who could land themselves in jail. That was their job and incarcerating or eliminating them was the shifters' job also. The shifter couldn't end up in a human jail. Not when the humans didn't know their kind existed and they had to keep it that way.

"None of the men were wearing hunter's spray, right?" He'd run into that a lot when trying to track down rogue shifters. Not always, but when they planned a criminal activity, they would often wear hunter's concealment to keep from being identified. Unless it was a crime of passion. Not that he could smell anything like the shifter agents could.

"No. I think this was something that was done on the spur of the moment. Let's split up and look for their clothes or a vehicle nearby." Justine got a call. "David? My new partner is here. Yeah, we're going to look for articles of clothing and a vehicle they might have driven here in. All right. Thanks. We'll keep you in mind. We appreciate it. Bye." She ended the call. "David said that everyone was working on cases of their own, but if we needed help, something like this took priority and they'd do whatever they could to assist us. But I think we have it covered for now."

"It's good that David and the others are living in the area and found the wounded men instead of someone else—human type —and reported this to the police."

"Right."

The ground was covered in a half a foot of snow, so they easily could follow the wolves' footprints. He didn't need the shifters' sense of smell for that. They found the men's clothes hidden in a pile of snow, though it was Justine who knew just where to look for them that time. And she had to be the one who told him they smelled the same as the men had who had been injured.

Then she put the clothes in an evidence bag, and he was glad she had her car equipped with all that.

They began to follow a hikers' boot prints back to a trail that cut off from the main road and he suspected they'd find a vehicle there, but they didn't.

"When were the men injured?" Rowdy asked, continuing to walk along the trail, but he figured it was futile. That the men wouldn't have parked that far away from where they hiked into the woods. In fact, there were no tire tracks this way. "No tire tracks. They parked back there."

Snowflakes were falling from the cloudy sky, and he breathed in the forest. He might not have the wolves' heightened sense of smell, but he loved smelling winter and pine trees and firs.

Seemingly ignoring him, Justine was headed for the road. He sighed. She probably thought he was an idiot, but it was his process. He would be thinking of things and people always mistook that as meaning he was a little absentminded, but it wasn't that. He was just mulling over different scenarios.

"Did David have any idea when the men might have been injured?" Rowdy asked again.

"Last night some time. They were in their wolf coats still, or they would have frozen to death."

He frowned at her. "Did you want me to carry all those clothes?"

She turned to look at him.

"You're in charge. I can—"

She frowned at him. "Yes, I'm in charge, but just like Everett calls the shots at the branch in Houston, he still helps with everything, including carrying evidence bags, doesn't he?"

Rowdy smiled. "Yeah. He's one of us in every way, listens to what we all think and half the time someone else comes up with a plan, and he goes along with it. If we're undecided, he'll wing it."

"What about you?" She continued to hike toward the road.

"Me?"

"Do you come up with plans to handle an investigation?"

"Yeah. I might not have your sense of smell, but I worked in homicide long enough that I've usually got a plan." He hoped he hadn't offended her, making her think she shouldn't have to carry the evidence bags because she was a woman. He was just thinking she was in charge, and he was perfectly fine being her gopher for the time-being.

"Good. That's just what I wanted to hear," she said.

They reached the road and looked both ways. "If there was one jaguar and he stole the wolves' car, he must have had his own vehicle too and had to move it," Rowdy said.

"That's just what I was thinking. Or he had someone else with him. Were they injured by one or two jaguars? Motivation? Why would he or they even fight the wolves? One jaguar came into the woods that I can smell," Justine said. "But you're right. Someone else had to be involved."

4

———————

Justine hadn't believed she'd be so glad to have a human partner, but Rowdy thought just like her while investigating a crime scene and two heads were better than one. Not to mention how impressed she was when he had responded so quickly and saved Kenny from drowning.

Then she got a call, looked at her phone and sighed. Her mom. Both her mom and dad were eager to meet the temporarily loaned special agent and she knew they thought she might fall for the guy and mate him. Which might have been a possibility if he had been a wolf!

"Yeah, uhm, Mom, we're investigating a case of a jaguar chewing up two wolf shifters."

"Oh, no. But the new guy is there to help you, right?" her mother asked, sounding a little worried.

"Yes, Rowdy and I are combing the woods for more clues, and then we'll be checking in with the injured men. We'll have to question them and discover exactly what had happened."

"Okay, well as soon as you have time, we want you both to come and have dinner with us. Or lunch. Whichever works best on your schedule."

"We're in the middle of an investigation." Justine had really thought she'd made that clear.

"I know dear, but you can't work it all night long. You have to eat. Dinner it is then. See you at six, if you can make it by then."

"All right. We'll make it for six." Justine ended the call with her mom and said to Rowdy, "We have a dinner date with my parents at six."

Rowdy raised his brows. "You're a gray wolf, right? I suspect they are too. I'm human. What will they think of that? Unless you've already told them."

"We *are* gray wolves. Sorry. I keep thinking you can smell me. And no, I haven't told them about you." She smiled brightly at him. "And I'm not going to tell them. They've been on my case about finding a nice wolf to settle down with. This is a great way to show them you're not available and they won't be pushing me to make something more of this than just working together on cases." This was a good way to assure Rowdy that she had no intention of turning him—to mate him or not. Though she wished he was a wolf and things might have been a whole lot different between them.

"You don't think they will have a fit when they see I'm human?" Rowdy sounded a little uncomfortable with the idea.

"Nah, believe me, they'll be shocked—like I was, but they'll be on their best behavior. They've been pushing me to check out a white wolf—pilot type—who flies passengers sightseeing over the Boundary Waters Canoe Area Wilderness, also dropping some off to go paddling. I intend to, I just haven't had time." Or the inclination. She could imagination some hotshot pilot interested in all kinds of women, even if she was thinking of him in a cliched way. "Anyway, they won't say a word about dating a wolf in front of you and my mom won't be making wedding plans for us either."

"Of course you want to see a wolf who lives and works here.

It sounds perfect." Rowdy didn't sound happy about it. "What will you say about me working for the USF as a special agent? Maybe your parents will suspect you requested me to work with you and have a thing for me already, more than you're willing to let on to them."

For a minute, she pondered the notion. Then she shook her head. "No. They know me better than that. Besides, when I asked Martin for help until he could hire someone, I didn't have any idea who he was sending, and I'd told my parents that."

"All right, but for the sake of argument, why not just tell your mom I'm human and it wouldn't work out between us. Wouldn't they suspect something is up because you're hiding the fact that I'm human from them?"

She arched a brow.

He smiled. Charming and disarming in the flesh, just like in his photos.

"No, they'll know I'm trying to prove a point and you wouldn't be an eligible bachelor for me, just a partner trying to solve crimes or aid shifters in trouble. Besides, you don't have anything else better to do with your time for dinner. Unless you really don't want to meet my parents because you might feel uncomfortable about being around them."

"Not at all. I'm more worried your parents might feel uncomfortable when they learn what I am. We can take separate vehicles in case they are upset."

Justine shook her head. "They would be mortified if you left early because of them. No, I'll drive us there." If her parents acted badly, she wouldn't want to stay any longer either.

When they didn't find anything further in their search for evidence in the woods, she motioned in the direction of her silver-blue Honda Civic Sport. "Let's go."

On the way over to the doctor's office, Rowdy was wearing

forensic gloves and went through the wolves' clothes. "No ID in any of their clothes."

"I didn't figure there would be any. Hopefully, we can ask them soon who they are and what happened. I just wish we knew what the jaguar looked like. There aren't any cameras in the area that would have captured images of them or their vehicles."

"Once we learn who the wolves are, we might be able to discover if they owned a vehicle that's been abandoned somewhere," Rowdy said.

"Right." She liked that Rowdy was always coming up with ideas of what they could check into further.

Then they finally arrived at the doctor's one-story, brick building and parked. It had been set up for emergency shifter cases and humans had no idea what it was really for. Just a sign out front that said, "Wolff, Inc."

Woods surrounded the property and mirrored glass windows allowed the viewer to look out, but anyone approaching the building couldn't see in. Anyone who had legitimate reasons to enter the building had to call ahead so they could be let inside. She had called already and when they arrived, the door automatically opened for them. As soon as they were inside with the wolves' clothes in hand, the door closed and locked.

The dark-haired receptionist smiled at them and said, "The doctor is in operating room, number three and you can go right in." But then she frowned at Rowdy, as if realizing he was human and he shouldn't be in there.

"Thanks," Justine said, and she and Rowdy headed down the hall.

"Have you been here before?" Rowdy asked as they walked past a couple of offices.

"No, but David told me how to make my way in here if I had

any need. I was hoping I wouldn't have any cases like this until I had more staff to assist me. I can't tell you enough how glad I am that you're here."

Rowdy smiled. "I'm glad to be here."

She probably would have had to get the private investigators' help with this if Rowdy hadn't come to aid her.

They entered the operating room where a redheaded doctor was sewing the first of the men up, a dark-haired nurse assisting.

"Dr. Roberts, this is Rowdy Sanderson. He works with the branch of USF down in Houston and is on loan to me for the time being," Justine said. "I'm Justine Winters."

Dr. Malcom Roberts glanced back at Rowdy, took a deep breath, and said, "He's human."

"He sure is. And he's a homicide detective and he knows how to work an investigation," Justine said, defending Rowdy. She'd never expected to have to do that for the agent, or that she'd feel obligated to do so.

"And he's working for a shifter organization, why?" Doc continued to sew up the man's wounds.

Rowdy was looking over the man too, examining the teeth marks at the wolf shifter's throat. If the jaguar hadn't held back, the man would have been dead. "I might not have your enhanced senses or the ability to grow wolf or jaguar teeth, but I have helped the shifter force in Houston solve any number of cases." He explained about the naked men that wolves had killed and how he had grown suspicious.

"If you want to bite him so he can officially be a wolf, be my guest," Justine said, motioning to Rowdy. "He wants to be one of us."

Doc glanced at Rowdy again and this time gave him a small smile.

"Yeah, anytime you want to, I'm game," Rowdy said, serious as could be.

Doc chuckled. The nurse was smiling too.

Justine was certain that wasn't going to be anything the doc would really consider doing. Someone who was newly turned needed to be watched to make sure he didn't have any shifting issues and give their kind all away.

She was beginning to feel badly that Rowdy wanted to be turned but no one would do that for him. Not that *she* had any intention of doing it to him, but still, she could see the dilemma he faced in having to explain why he was working with shifters all the time, trying to be accepted by them, even wanting to be accepted by her.

She decided that she was going to be super nice to him from now on. Not that she'd been mean to him so far, but she'd been feeling out of sorts that he was human, and she thought he wouldn't be all that helpful in an investigation.

"One jaguar bit into each of the men," Rowdy said, checking the other injured man, bandaged up already, and still out cold.

Both men were on IVs and were getting blood transfusions. They appeared to be heavily sedated.

"We need to know who all the players are," Justine said. "We need to notify the wolves' families too. So what was the motivation for attacking the two men?"

"They're vicious attacks," Rowdy said. "He was angry when he fought the men."

Doc nodded. "Yeah, that's my finding too. But the wolves tore into him too. They have plenty of his blood and fur in their mouths."

Rowdy was checking the second man's mouth. "I see. We need to learn who the instigator was. Can you get DNA from the blood?"

"Yeah, I sure will try. Even if I get anything off them, we might not be able to find the jaguars or these wolves in the database."

"When do you think they'll be ready to talk?" Justine asked.

"Their wounds are severe enough, that I had to heavily sedate them and they also lost a lot of blood. They'll live, but they won't be able to answer your questions for a while."

"Thanks, Doc. Let us know when they can talk. We brought their clothes so they can wear them once they're able to leave." Justine looked at Rowdy to see if he was ready to go.

He nodded, thanked the doctor, and then they headed out.

"So what do you think about motive?" she asked.

"Had the jaguar known the guys were hiking together and— no, their clothes weren't in the same location," Rowdy said. "There's no other disturbance of snow where the wolves' clothes were. If the jaguar and the wolves had gone together, they probably would have buried their clothes in the same location."

"Good point."

"So the jaguar had run into them and got into a fight? Randomly? He followed them there and fought them over an earlier beef? Or vice versa."

"Hmm, so we need to ask if anyone saw three men get into a confrontation somewhere. Like at a bar or something before they went into the woods. Maybe they planned to air their grievances as shifters, only the jaguars have a much stronger bite than the wolves and can leap into and out of trees. They are heavier too. I mean, a jaguar fighting a couple of wolves isn't a whole lot of competition for him. The wolves could have arrogantly believed they had a good chance at beating the jaguar."

"Except the jaguar took it too far. Neither side backing down," Rowdy said, as she drove them back to the office. "Or the jaguar didn't make it."

"Not a good scenario. Okay, so there's one place I know of where bear shifters go. I'm not sure about wolves or jaguar shifters, but we can check out the pub and see if anyone recognizes either of the wolves," she said.

"That sounds like a good idea."

When they got back to the office, Rowdy was checking out the Christmas decorations.

She'd set up a Christmas tree and decorated it with a mixture of animals—wolves primarily, bears, cougars, foxes, and jaguars.

"I tried to find some animals to decorate the tree to represent the different shifters we might encounter. I don't know for sure if there are fox shifters, but I love them. I've run into a cougar shifter once. And I've heard that a caraco exists."

"I wouldn't be surprised if there are," Rowdy said.

The tree was situated in front of the window so that it could be enjoyed both inside the building and outside. Christmas lights were strung up around the outside of the building and on the inside. She'd even got him some poinsettias for his office.

"I love the decorations," he said. "They're nice and festive."

"Thanks. I love Christmas. So decorating the offices makes me feel like I'm celebrating the season at my home away from home when I'm here."

"I agree. I feel like that too when we decorated the offices back in Houston. We even have door-decorating contests."

She glanced at their office doors, then smiled at him.

He thought it was kind of late to do one here before Christmas. "We decorate the tree together, hang lights. It's all part of being a team. And of course, we're playing Christmas music and drinking eggnog when we do it."

"Now that sounds like fun. I love your Argyle sweater. It makes me think of skiing."

"I had to bring out all my sweaters and a heavy coat for this trip."

"I bet." Then she helped him log into the office computer. He had his own office as a special agent. She hadn't hired a secretary yet because jobs were hit and miss, but the more people knew about her being here and ready to help their kind, the more calls she was getting in. So she would have to hire someone to begin fielding calls soon, she figured.

"While we're waiting for the wolves to come out of sedation, do you want to visit the pub?" Rowdy asked.

"Yeah, let's go."

5

J ustine and Rowdy soon arrived at the pub. A few early arrivals were already drinking. "A couple of bears," Justine said low for Rowdy's ears. "The rest are humans."

"Do you know them?"

"No, but I can smell their scents. The two we just passed, the burly guys, are bears." Then Justine sat on a barstool and ordered a soda.

Rowdy did too.

White and gold lights decorated the pub, a Christmas tree in one corner was filled with plain red, green, and white bows and wooden and fabric bears. A large hand-carved bear stood poised with teeth bared next to the bar as if it were the bouncer for the establishment. She'd figured it was a bear establishment once she'd seen it.

When the bartender, who was a bear—black-haired, six-four, and bearded—brought their drinks, he smiled at Justine, but frowned at Rowdy, probably because she was with a human.

"We're with the United Shifter Force," she said low to the bartender. "We're looking into a fight between a jaguar and a couple of wolves."

"He's with you?" the bartender asked, motioning with his head in Rowdy's direction.

"Yeah. He works with our force." She introduced them and the bartender said he was Bran McConnell, his clear green eyes focused again on Rowdy.

"It can't be easy for you when you can't even tell if any of us are shifters," Bran told Rowdy.

"That's why I'm eager for someone to bite me."

Bran smiled. "You rile up a drunk bear in here and he's liable to bite you. But you might not live through the ordeal."

"He wants to be a wolf," Justine explained.

Bran shook his head. "Bears are where it's at. So why haven't *you* turned him?"

"We just met," Rowdy said, not wasting any time to respond.

Bran smiled again. "Good luck with that." He said it to Rowdy, not to Justine.

"We're just working partners. You know the trouble wolves can have during the full moon phase," Justine said. "We wanted to know if you had seen wolves or jaguars in the place that could have been having issues with each other last night."

"Jaguars? No. But we did have a couple of raucous wolves in here who were pissing off bears and humans alike."

Justine showed him pictures of the men on her phone.

"Yeah, that's them. I had to bodily throw them out of here before they riled up too many more of my patrons." Bran snapped his fingers. "You're the woman who turned in a couple of our teens to our sleuth leader after they were breaking into beehives a couple of months ago. I heard all about it."

"We had to rescue them after they fell through the frozen lake today," Justine said. "Well, actually, Rowdy did."

"Knowing those two brothers? I believe it. They're good kids, if they get the right kind of guidance. I have to admit a lot of us go through the same phase. Some of us never grow out of it. If you need my help with anything, you've got it. I'll even turn you, Rowdy, if you ever decide to be one of us."

"Thanks for the information and for the offer," Rowdy said.

"No problem. I hope you catch the jaguar who was involved. I wouldn't think that would be a fair fight."

"You're right. The wolves are lucky he didn't kill them." Justine thanked him too and then they left the pub.

THAT NIGHT, Rowdy really wasn't sure about going to see Justine's parents. He could just imagine them being shocked into silence. He hoped that wouldn't be the case, but if he were a parent and he was hopeful his daughter would find a nice wolf to mate and she brought home a human instead, he wouldn't be happy. He really wanted to take his own vehicle in case he had to leave. But he went along with what she wanted, hoping this wasn't a mistake.

When they arrived at her parents' home, he realized it wasn't far from Justine's place on the lake. He admired the modest, one-story, red-brick home surrounded by snowy woods, Christmas candles in each of the windows, and Christmas lights hanging off the roof and around each of the windows, making it appear festive and welcoming. Even the path from the driveway to the house had little lights lighting the way. It didn't lessen his apprehension about meeting her parents though.

She knocked on the door and her mother answered it, her dark hair like Justine's, except peppered with silver, and the dad smiling from the open kitchen, a serving spoon in hand. "Just in time," he said.

Jingle Bells was playing in the background and the scent of cinnamon spice filled the air.

"My mom, Georgiana, Georgia for short, and my dad, Frank,

Francis, but no one calls him by that name," Justine said. "And this is Rowdy Sanderson, my temporary partner."

"Welcome," Georgia said, her smiling composure not slipping in the least even though she was close enough to Rowdy now as she took his coat and Justine's that he knew she smelled he was human. Her eyes were smiling with intrigue and the same pretty clear green as Justine's. "So how long will you be staying for?"

"As long as Justine needs me until Martin can hire someone to help her out," Rowdy said, relaxing a little.

"Good. We worried that she'd bitten off more than she could chew when she had no one to help her with cases. Come in and tell us a little bit about yourself."

Rowdy liked Georgia. He knew she had to be surprised to learn he was human, but she truly was welcoming, no airs about it. He shook Frank's extended hand. He was dark haired also, but his eyes were more amber than green.

"I'm glad to be here to help all I can." Rowdy explained where he had come from before he worked in Houston and how he came to work with the wolves and jaguars. And of course, that he wanted to be a wolf like them, though he knew wolf shifters were reluctant to deal with a newly turned wolf.

He was glad the dad hadn't reacted any differently than the mother, seemingly fine that Rowdy was human. Maybe it really didn't matter to them as long as he watched Justine's back and helped keep her safe while she was working.

"You know those Arctic wolves in the area were newly turned, or at least the four private investigators were and so were two of their mates," Georgia said, buttering a roll. "Once we met them, we were delighted to make new friends and they were grateful to meet more of their kind. I couldn't imagine how they survived on their own until they had more of a handle on their shifting. They hadn't chosen to be bitten either. I think you're courageous to want to be one of us."

Maybe making friends with the white wolves was the reason Justine's parents were fine with it. "I know a couple of the Arctic wolves already."

"That's great. We're so glad you're here," Frank said. "How do you like Minnesota?"

"I've liked what I've seen so far. I'm really more of a winter-weather person than a hot-weather person, so I really felt at home when I began to see snow."

"Oh, us, too," Georgia said.

"And I love outdoor activities, so I hope to go water rafting and paddling when it's viable, though I might not be here that long if Martin hires someone else for the job." Rowdy knew his boss was working hard to find someone for Justine's branch to partner up with her.

"So what is the deal with this new case you're working on?" Frank asked.

Rowdy figured they'd bring it up. Everyday no problem cases were one thing, but a jaguar shifter who could have easily killed the two wolves? That was an entirely different matter.

"My dad is a retired insurance fraud investigator, and he is always interested in solving criminal cases," Justine said as they took their seats at an oak table and began passing around dinner rolls, a large serving bowl of mashed potatoes, another of carrots, gravy, and a platter of prime rib roast.

Already Rowdy's stomach was grumbling, and everyone smiled at him, courtesy of their wolf hearing.

"Eat up before the food gets cold," Georgia said.

Justine told her parents what they'd found so far, but they didn't have much to go on.

"Remember we have the Christmas wrapping activity

tomorrow morning for the charity event for kids, right, Justine?" Georgia asked.

"Oh, Mom, I'd forgotten about it, what with this new case and all."

"Well, we want Rowdy to come too," Georgia said.

"But we have this deadly business to take care of," Justine said.

"I can keep working on it while you're wrapping presents," Rowdy offered. "That's part of the great thing about me being here. If you have something else to do, I can continue to look for clues."

She gave him a dark look and he suspected she was glad to have something that would keep her from having to wrap presents.

"Nonsense," Georgia said. "Unless you have a lead to track down and the bad guys might get away during that time, both of you should come and help. In fact, if you do, it will take half the time to do it. Two hours max, maybe an hour, depending on how fast the two of you wrap." Georgia smiled.

"It's our annual gig," Frank said. "Once I retired, there was no getting out of it."

Justine laughed then. "You always took off to help us. It was a family affair to spread some Christmas cheer."

"Yeah, sure, I'll help." Rowdy didn't want to sound like a Scrooge at Christmastime.

"Excellent!" Georgia said. "And we have a Christmas party to attend on Sunday night at the lake where the Arctic wolves have their homes. Wolf run, great food, Christmas games, if Justine didn't tell you about it yet."

Justine frowned at her mother for mentioning the wolf run because obviously Rowdy wasn't a wolf.

"Uh, she didn't, but then I just drove in from Houston today." Rowdy smiled. "I know Owen Nottingham and his mate,

Candice." He explained the avalanche story again and how he knew the white dogs reported to have rescued the sledders were really Arctic wolves, which wouldn't have lived in the area that the accident occurred.

"Oh, wow, that's great. You must be tired from that long drive."

"He has to be," Justine said, not allowing him to deny it. "That's a twenty-two-hour drive and he arrived before noon. Then he had to rescue the boys from the lake." She explained all about that adventure.

Though Rowdy had only had to rescue Kenny. Both her parents seemed impressed, and he felt good about earning the wolf shifters' respect.

"Those boys sure do get themselves into trouble," Georgia said.

Frank carved up some more of his prime rib. "I can't believe we were out doing some last-minute Christmas shopping when that happened, or we would have been there to help."

"I thought you were done—" Justine abruptly stopped and smiled. "Okay, yeah, I need to do a bit more too."

"Where are you staying while you're here, Rowdy?" Georgia asked.

"In a cabin owned by wolves on Birch Lake. I'm going to love it there."

"Oh, my, yes. You'll enjoy it," Georgia agreed.

They finally finished eating dinner and then said their good nights. On the way back to the office so Rowdy could pick up his car and head back to his cabin, Justine said, "Sorry you got rooked into helping us to wrap Christmas presents. I had hoped that with this case pending, my mom would realize we might be busy. But when I took this job here, Mom had her heart set on doing this as a family again."

Which reminded Rowdy of how close wolf pack families could be. "I don't mind at all."

"Good. Oh, and I didn't know what to expect concerning their reaction to you being human, but I told you they would be nice about it."

"Yeah, I guess it helped that your parents like the newly turned white wolves in the area." And that gave him an idea. What if he could convince one of *them* to turn him?

"It did." Justine sighed. "I swear my mother was even considering biting you when you told them your story."

He chuckled. "I wouldn't be averse to it."

"That's what I would be afraid of."

When they finally arrived at the office, Justine said good night to him.

Then he headed home and thought the day was a success. He was becoming part of the wolf shifter community here and earning a good reputation among the bears too. He liked working for Justine. And he liked her parents. In fact, he suspected Georgia was ready to turn him so that he could be an eligible bachelor wolf for Justine, in case she didn't want to turn him herself. But still, he thought the best chance he might have of being turned was to see Owen and Candice again. Of course, if one of them bit him, he would be a white wolf then, not a gray. He thought he could blend in better with the local wolf population as a gray wolf.

He parked at his cabin and saw two brown bears, one a little darker than the other, both of them not fully grown, and they saw him and hightailed it into the woods. One looked suspiciously like Andrew.

They had to be shifters. Regular bears would be hibernating this time of year in Minnesota. He headed inside his cabin and thought he had made the best decision he could have in volunteering to work with Justine, though he hadn't expected the agent to be a woman, a beautiful woman, who appeared to be just as detail oriented as him on a mission. If he'd had a wolf's night vision, he would have gone back to the scene of the crime and looked for more evidence, but that would have to wait until first light tomorrow.

AT HER HOME THAT NIGHT, Justine took a shower and thought about Rowdy and the impression he'd made on her parents. The *good* impression he'd made. If he hadn't, they wouldn't have mentioned her wrapping presents and invited him to come along, or to come to a wolf party that would be shifter attendees only. She was glad he knew a couple of the Arctic wolves though. That should help him feel more at ease among them. She was proud of her parents for being so open minded also.

She would tell Cameron and Faith MacPherson, the wolves who were in charge of the white wolf pack, that she was bringing Rowdy to the party. She wanted him to enjoy himself like she planned to. And maybe she could meet that hotshot bachelor wolf pilot too. She hoped Rowdy would mingle and get to know everyone so she wouldn't have to feel she needed to be with him every minute of the night.

She dried off and then threw on a long, Christmas gnome T-shirt and called Faith. "Hi, this is Justine and I wanted to let you know that I'm bringing the agent that the Houston branch loaned to me to the party. He's human. Rowdy Sanderson. Owen and Candice know him."

"Ohmigod, yes! He's here? We can't wait to meet him."

6

J ustine couldn't believe it when Rowdy joined her in the woods at dawn to look for anything important at the crime scene. She had only arrived about ten minutes before that. She had assumed he wouldn't get into the office until eight, when they normally worked, unless they had a lead.

"I didn't expect you to come out here," she said, finding a blood trail she hadn't seen yesterday.

"I watched the sunrise on the lake, then headed right over. I suspected you would be here."

She smiled at him, appreciating the compliment. "I missed this blood trail yesterday."

"I did too. In fact, if you hadn't pointed it out, I probably would have missed it today too. Can you smell what it was that left the blood?"

"A jaguar. So he must have been injured in the fight. I'm not surprised since there were two wolves and they can hold their own for a while, but the jaguars' bites are killing machines. They can bite through a tortoise shell they're so strong. When you worked with the jaguars and wolves, you must have actually witnessed fights like that, right?"

"I did. The jaguars took on the rogue jaguars. The wolves were acting as bait."

"I imagine you felt left out."

"I wish I could have helped more, that's for certain. Like the situation with this blood. I might have smelled it before you had pointed it out to me if I were a shifter."

They continued to search the area, and this time Rowdy found some jaguar fur on a thorny bush. He bagged it. "If we don't get any DNA evidence off the bites on the wolves, maybe this will give us some DNA."

"If he's in the system."

"Right. You know I keep thinking the jaguar was the aggressor, but it's entirely possible that the wolves were the stalkers and attacked him."

"True, though they would have to be crazy to do so." Justine got a call from the doctor then. "What did you learn?" She put it on speakerphone so Rowdy could listen in.

"The blood alcohol toxicology report came back—.13 percent. Loss of judgement can occur, slurring of words, obvious physical impairment."

"Okay, so they were inebriated, probably after going to the pub and being so antagonistic there that they had to be tossed out and could have started a fight with a jaguar they couldn't finish. Especially if the jaguar was drunk too."

"There was nothing we could find in any databases that showed the jaguars were in the system."

"So you had enough DNA evidence from the saliva," Rowdy said.

"Some."

"We've got some jaguar fur. Maybe it has some roots that will give us an indication of who he was. And I've collected a few blood drops, so the jaguar was injured," she said.

"Okay, drop those by when you have time. Also, I called to tell you the wolves are awake, but I couldn't get anything out of them," the doctor said.

"We'll be right over," Justine said.

When she and Rowdy couldn't find anything else in the woods, they dropped off the new evidence with the doctor and then he led them to the room where the men were staying.

The doctor folded his arms across his chest. "They intended to leave, but we need to learn what happened, so I had to have them restrained. The fair-haired man is Roger Cummings and the other is Fenwick Livingston."

"Thanks, Doc." Justine was glad he had confined them because she could imagine them taking off and this would be an unsolved case then. She brought out a recorder. "Tell us exactly what happened."

Roger frowned at her. "A jaguar attacked us, obviously."

"Did you know who the jaguar was?"

"Hell, no. It was an unprovoked attack. We're innocent and here we're zip tied to the beds as if we were the ones at fault." Fenwick looked just as growly.

Both men were badly bruised and bandaged.

"Did you notify family?" Rowdy asked the doctor.

"They said they have no family and they're not from around here," Doc said.

"Okay, so you were both inebriated when the fight occurred," Justine said.

"That's why the jaguar took advantage of us," Fenwick said.

"What were you doing in the woods?" she asked.

"We were going to take a run as wolves and then this jaguar came out of nowhere," Roger said.

"And your car? What happened to it?"

Both men looked at each other and then Fenwick quickly said, "The driver of the other vehicle slammed into my pickup and totaled it."

Justine suspected that wasn't the case or they would have mentioned that first and not told the story about just going for a wolf run, besides the fact that Fenwick and his friend had been drunk.

"So the driver of the vehicle was a jaguar? The one who fought with you in the woods?" Rowdy asked.

"Yeah," Fenwick said.

"What happened to his car?" Rowdy took pictures of both men.

"Hell if we know," Roger said.

"Okay, so the vehicles collided—"

"He rammed us," Roger said.

Since the men had already lied about some of the details, she assumed it was the other way around, unless the jaguar had been drinking over the limit also. "You get out of your vehicles and then what? You all shift to go for a run?" Justine figured they'd fought as humans, exchanged verbal threats, then shifted and tore into each other in the woods.

"We got out of my vehicle and approached the other guy's car." Fenwick let out his breath in exasperation. "We had to exchange insurance information and shit."

"And things got out of hand, and you shifted, he shifted, and you fought in the woods." Justine assumed it since he seemed hesitant to tell the whole story.

"There was no making peace with the big cat. He claimed the accident was Fenwick's fault and…" Roger shrugged.

"You shifted and fought, but you had sense enough to leave the road first so no one would see you shifting and fighting." Though she wondered if the jaguar had moved the confrontation to the woods since she figured these guys hadn't been thinking with a clear head.

"Yeah, if we hadn't, that fool jaguar would have fought us right on the road!" Fenwick shook his head.

She suspected the wolves had been too drunk to make that decision.

Fenwick frowned. "Did you tow my truck?"

"Someone did," Rowdy said. "It was gone when we arrived."

"But you found him and us, right?" Roger pulled at the restraints, looking irritated that he was confined.

"He was gone, the vehicles were gone. Only the two of you had remained behind," Rowdy said.

"So he's hiding, guilty, just like we said he was." Fenwick glanced at Roger, and he nodded.

"We won't know for sure until we get *his* side of the story," Rowdy said.

"Hell, he committed a hit and run then." Fenwick smiled a little.

True, it did mean he left the scene of the crime, though if the wolves were the fault of it all, that was a different story.

"We need your addresses, phone numbers, and the place you're staying right now." Justine hoped they'd at least be honest with her about that.

"We're just passing through, pulled up stakes and driving around the country, looking for someplace else to settle," Roger said.

"Former pack?"

Fenwick cleared his throat. "Loners."

Justine didn't trust anything he said. She wondered if they were with a pack that had chased them out, or that they were in trouble with and they ran before they could be dealt with. She knew of some packs around the states, maybe the Arctic wolf pack knew of some too and she'd send word about the two men.

"Former address?" she asked.

"Just been traveling," Fenwick said.

"Okay, fine." It meant more work locating where they were from, but she'd send out the word.

Rowdy raised his brows. "Sounds to me like you've got something to hide."

"What the hell is a human doing here anyway?" Roger asked. "Since you obviously know about our kind, you should have been eliminated."

Rowdy smiled. "The way I see it is that you're on the run, were drunk, totaled the jaguar's car, started the fight, belligerent like you were in the pub you visited the night beforehand and the bartender had to toss you out, and if anyone should possibly be eliminated, I'd certainly vote for you."

Fenwick scowled. "You wouldn't have a vote, human."

"No, but I would," Justine said, "and I agree with my partner."

Doc inclined his head. "I'd have to agree with the special agents too."

"Okay, we'll be talking to you again," Justine said.

"Wait, you can't hold us here." Fenwick jerked at his restraints.

"Yes, I have the authority until we know who's at fault. Since you won't tell us where you're from or anything much about yourselves, you're a flight risk." Then Justine waited for Rowdy to say anything further.

"We'll turn them over to the jaguars' holding facility soon," Rowdy said to the doctor. "No sense having them tying up a couple of beds if they don't need any further medical care."

"You can't lock us up in the jaguar confinement facility," Fenwick said, but Rowdy and Justine were already leaving the room.

"Time to wrap Christmas presents." Justine hoped Rowdy really was okay with it. "Are you ready?"

Rowdy got the door for her as they said goodbye to the receptionist. "Yep. I thought we could send out the word about the two wolves and see if any of the packs had heard of them."

"That's exactly what I was planning to do. Between the two of us, and others we know, we might be able to find someone who knows them."

Then they finally arrived at the center where volunteers were busily wrapping presents of all sizes. Justine looked over at Rowdy. "You know you're really a good sport about this."

"Well, I don't know how good I will be at wrapping things, but I'm all for helping social causes, especially during the holidays."

Justine's parents saw them and came over to talk to them. Her mom hugged both Justine and then Rowdy and motioned to a table they could go to.

Frank shook Rowdy's hand and slapped him on the back in a hearty greeting. "It's really not all that bad, once you learn how to wrap presents correctly."

Rowdy laughed. "I'm ready."

Then he and Justine took their seats at one of the tables, but before they began wrapping presents, they shared notes about which packs they knew of. Then they began to share the pictures of the men with the packs. Mission came first.

Once they were done, Justine glanced at Rowdy as he wrapped a doll in a box. "You're really good at that."

"Thanks. Mom told me I was the worst present wrapper ever and so she taught me how to use less tape, fold edges, and create envelope corners on the ends of boxes."

Justine laughed. "I had to learn how to do this when I started wrapping presents with my parents as a team." She paused in her wrapping. "Hey, listen, Christmas is next week, and you have to come over and have Christmas Eve dinner and the turkey with us on Christmas Day. I should have asked you earlier, but I'd forgotten about it."

He wrapped another package. "I sure will. Thanks. I had dinner offers from the jaguars and the wolves back home, but then I came up here. I figured I'd manage to fix something, but it would be really special to have it with you and your family." He paused. "You know, last night I had a couple of bear shifters come by my cabin. Teens, I think. They weren't full grown. Fully grown bears would be hibernating. So I figured they had to be shifters. And I thought the one looked like Andrew, but I couldn't be certain. He had been wet, and his fur was darker than the bears I saw."

Frowning, Justine stopped wrapping the present she was halfway finished with and pulled out her cell phone. "I have the teens' pictures I took when they were bears raiding beehives." She found the pictures and handed Rowdy her phone. "Does this look like them?"

Rowdy studied the photos. "Could be. I'm not an expert on bears."

"They all look the same, right?"

He chuckled. "Yeah, something like that."

"So what were they doing?"

"I don't know. Checking me out? I think."

She narrowed her eyes. "Why?"

"I found bear fur by the shifter door of the cabin. Martin recommended I stay there and called the owners with a heads-up to let them know I work with shifters. They gave me the cabin by the edge of the woods. More private. Perfect if I'd been a shifter."

"Or perfect for teen bear shifters to skulk around your cabin." She began working on her present again.

"Yeah. I wonder what they were up to. If I'd been a shifter, I would have chased after them."

She sighed. "If I turned you—"

"Hell, yeah! Seriously?"

"I would never have considered doing it for an ordinary human, but seeing how you work with shifters and the disadvantage you're at in working with us, knowing what we are, having to always explain yourself to us…"

"You'd have a partner for life. I mean, to work here. You wouldn't be burdened with having to take me as a mate. I'd be able to do so much more."

She laughed. "We take a mate for life." She showed him the pictures on her phone that Martin had sent her of him shirtless, his muscles glistening with sweat, and he was giving the person who took the pictures of him a sexy, little smirk.

Rowdy frowned at them. "Who sent these to you?"

"Martin. He said that one of his she-cats put them in your personal file."

Rowdy laughed. "*This* is all you had of me to judge me by when here I'm going to be working for you?"

She smiled. "I figured you would be really handy if we had to lift anything heavy—like pulling a teen bear out of a partially frozen lake."

He chuckled.

Then she glanced in the direction of the entryway. "Speak of the devils."

7

Wondering who the devils were that Justine was talking about, Rowdy looked at the doorway and saw two teens walk into the room.

"Andrew and Kenny Brixworth. What are they doing here?" Justine asked.

"Maybe their dad is making them wrap presents for losing his truck in the lake," Rowdy said.

The boys headed straight for their wrapping table, and she wondered if Rowdy was right. "Did you come to wrap presents?"

"We—" Andrew said.

"Yeah, we did." Kenny eyed Rowdy with suspicion.

"Were you at Rowdy's cabin last night?" Justine asked.

Andrew sighed. "Busted. We saw you together."

"Where?"

"Going to the doctor's office. We—" Andrew said.

Kenny cleared his throat. "We saw a jaguar fighting wolves in the woods where we were planning to run the other night."

"Seriously? Pull up some chairs and help us wrap presents," Justine said.

Andrew grabbed an empty chair and joined them at the

table. "Dad told us to come and talk to you about it while helping to wrap presents because, uh, we—"

Kenny pulled up a chair and started to wrap a present. "We lost his truck in the lake and we weren't supposed to be out running the other night."

"It was more than that," Andrew said.

Kenny nodded. "Yeah, we went to the pub and saw the drunken men there."

"You weren't supposed to be in the pub," Rowdy guessed.

"Right. So then the two drunk wolves left the pub and we asked if we could drive them somewhere and they said no," Andrew said.

Kenny cut off some wrapping paper. "They got in their truck and weaved all over the road. Then they smashed up a car and both vehicles spun out of control and went off the road. We drove down the road a way, then decided we had to go back and check things out. Make sure no one was dying.

"We pulled the pickup off the road, got out, and hurried back to where the wrecked vehicles were. We didn't see anyone there. We thought maybe the drivers and passengers were badly hurt and walked into the woods, but then we heard fighting and saw a jaguar and the wolves tearing into each other. We tore off, not wanting to get chewed up. We thought that they were just getting their aggressions out because of the car wreck."

Andrew said, "We didn't tell anyone about it because we weren't supposed to be at the pub—"

"Or driving the truck out that late," Kenny said.

"And you'd be grounded again. Why were you at Rowdy's cabin?" Justine asked.

"We heard the wolves had been badly injured and we saw Rowdy with you at the clinic. So we figured you knew about the fight. We thought maybe we wouldn't be in as much trouble if we talked to him than if we talked to you since you already caught us at the beehives." Andrew smiled. "And because he saved Kenny."

"Yeah, we had a change of heart when we saw Rowdy, figuring he would be sore with us, and we took off." Kenny glanced at Rowdy. "Thanks for saving me, by the way."

"You're welcome."

"What do we do about this now?" Kenny asked.

"You two do nothing. But we need to know if you caught the numbers on their license plates or anything else that would help us," Rowdy said.

"A partial," Andrew said, and gave it to them.

"Jaguar's car or the wolves' truck?" Justine asked.

"The jaguar's. A yellow Nissan Altima. But it wasn't the jaguars' fault, we don't think," Kenny said. "The wolves had been quarrelsome at the pub. That's what our dad always calls us when Andrew and I fight. Quarrelsome. They were drunk. The bartender threw them out, then saw us in the pub and made us leave. The wolves wrecked the other vehicle, and they had a pickup truck, unfair advantage. And then things got really out of hand."

"Thanks for finally telling us," Justine said.

"We're sorry we didn't tell you earlier," Kenny said.

"Yeah, we got heck for that too," Andrew said.

Then everyone hunkered down to get the Christmas wrapping done, but Justine and Rowdy left after an hour and a half to look into the partial license plate number for the car that the jaguar had been driving.

"They seem to always be getting themselves into trouble of one kind or another," Justine said as they headed back to the office.

"They remind me of me at that age."

"There's hope for the boys yet then."

"Exactly."

"So what made you become a homicide detective?" she asked.

"A good friend of mine was murdered in college, and I didn't feel the homicide detectives were looking into the right suspect. I began following the guy who had done some handyman stuff around his parents' home and the police had interviewed him, but he had an airtight alibi. I wasn't buying it. His mother said he was at home sleeping, and she'd swear to it.

"I didn't believe her, but without hard evidence to prove otherwise, the police wouldn't do anything else about him and went after another possible suspect who had no alibi. Someone my friend had fought with over a girlfriend. Sure, the guy was a hothead, but I knew he would never have killed him. I was following the one I suspected did the killing. When I saw him trying to kill another college student after that, I notified the police. This time, they really looked into his story and found enough evidence to prove he had done the murder and attempted murder on the second guy."

"What was his motivation?"

"With the first case, my friend saw this guy breaking into his parents' home and he killed him for it. In the second case, he had a fight with the guy and tried to kill him. He had gotten away with it once. Why not again? So what made you become a police detective?"

"My dad was an insurance fraud investigator. But he couldn't arrest the wrongdoers, only hand over evidence to the police. I wanted to actually put the handcuffs on them."

Rowdy smiled.

"Seriously." She found the record for the jaguar's car. "Okay, we have a Mason Talbot, owner of the yellow car out of Tomball, Texas."

"That's near Houston. I'll call Everett and ask if they can run down any leads there." As soon as Rowdy got hold of Everett, he put the call on speakerphone. "Justine's here with me. We're trying to learn what we can about a Mason Talbot." He explained why.

"We'll see what we can come up with. I've never heard of the jaguar myself personally, but we'll get back with you as soon as we learn anything."

"Thanks, Everett. We appreciate it."

"Sure thing. How are things going for you there?"

"Great. I rescued a teen bear shifter from a lake today, and now we've got this wolves-versus-jaguar's case going on, so a great start already. And I might even have some luck at convincing a wolf to turn me."

Everett laughed. "Good luck with that."

"Thanks."

"Wait, does that mean you might not be returning to us?"

Rowdy glanced at Justine. She only just smiled.

"I have no idea," Rowdy said.

"Well, we'll really miss you if you do and I know more than a few will wish they had turned you already so we could have kept you here."

"Yeah, well, we'll have to see what happens. Let us know if you find anything on Mason, will you? We need to find this guy and get his story."

"Will do, and great news on the other front. Talk later."

Then they ended the call and Rowdy sighed. "I guess I should have asked you first if it was okay to mention a wolf possibly turning me."

Justine smiled. "I know how much this means to you. We can do it after the party tomorrow night, if you still want to do it." She figured she'd let them both sleep on it. Maybe now that someone had finally said she'd turn him, he would get cold feet about it. It was a big change to go through, though he seemed to understand them well enough, not like what had happened to the Arctic wolves who had been clueless.

Rowdy would have a lot of wolves who could guide him through the changes. She considered what it would be like to run her hands over all those hard muscles and kiss him senseless. She might have to even claim him for her own and keep him for good—not just as a partner—when did she give up the part about being in charge of the branch?

But with him, she already wanted to be his partner and not his boss, and that was a huge thing for her to concede. So why not a partner in all things?

Before he left to return to his cabin that night, Rowdy said, "I picked up a couple of steaks for dinners when I was at the grocery store if you'd like to join me and watch the sunset. A little different than on your side of the lake. If you don't have any plans."

"You know, I'd like that." She had planned to have a chicken breast and baked potato tonight, but having a steak with a hot wannabe wolf and watch the sun set at White Birch Resort? Yeah, that sounded like fun. And she liked that he had offered. "I'll just follow you over there."

Before long, they were sitting at his kitchen table and having steaks topped with sautéed mushrooms and crumbled blue cheese, mashed potatoes, and asparagus.

"This really hit the spot." She finished off the last of her steak. "Really delicious." She liked a man who knew how to cook.

"I'm glad you enjoyed dinner." He made them hot cups of chocolate topped with whipped cream afterward and they bundled up and took the wooden steps to the bottom of the hilltop cabins. They took a seat on a log bench to finish watching the sun set, the colors reflecting cherry and purple off the clouds and across the water.

"This is really beautiful. Though the sun setting on my lake is too. And we'll get to see the sunset on the white wolves' lake tomorrow night. Their lake is even bigger than mine." She snuggled against Rowdy for warmth and because she wanted something more between them if she was going to turn him. What if he felt pressured to do something more with her just so he could win her favor and she would bite him though?

She gazed out at the darkening sky, the clouds drifting in, hiding the stars. She wanted to run with him as a wolf in the worst way tonight.

Before she could propose biting him, he leaned down and looked into her eyes, the question in his gaze saying he wanted to kiss her. He didn't forge ahead, maybe because she was his boss, or maybe because he didn't want to do something she wasn't ready for, but she was! She set her empty mug down on the ground and noticed he'd already done that with his. Then she reached up and pulled his face down to meet hers.

He went for a slow buildup, kissing her mouth with skill, judging her reaction, not taking advantage, but not ending the kiss either. Lips had more nerve endings than anywhere else in the body. and he sure was stimulating hers to perfection.

She groaned with need. No man had ever kissed her with such finesse. His exquisite touch filled her with affection and euphoria—courtesy of their heightened serotonin, dopamine, and oxytocin. Even though it had been cold out here, the wintry breeze from the lake sweeping across them, he was heating her blood to the max.

Then their mouths opened to each other, and tongues caressed in a mating dance. Oh, she was so into this. She finally broke off the kiss, but she didn't want to end this here.

"It's cold out here." Though she really wasn't feeling the cold, not with the way he was heating her up. "Let's take this inside."

"Yeah, sure." He helped her up and grabbed their mugs, then they made their way over the icy rocks to the stairs.

They finally reached the cabin and he set the mugs in the kitchen, and they stripped out of their parkas, gloves, and hats. Then she led him to his bedroom, the one where she had smelled his scent the strongest. She knew what she wanted. She hoped he was thinking along the same lines as her.

He slipped her red sweater over her head and tossed it aside. He slid his hands over her shoulders making them tingle with his touch and she lifted her chin, offering her lips to his for another soul-searing kiss.

This time he wasn't holding back, the passion of his warm mouth against hers exciting her, spurring her on. She slipped her hands beneath his soft navy sweater and ran them up his hot abs. Man, was he exquisite. A body built for loving. Her loving.

Yeah, she was going to bite him. Forget waiting until tomorrow night. And then she was going to keep him as long as things worked out like she thought they would between them.

He would get his long-awaited Christmas present. She would get hers. And so would her parents. Martin wouldn't have to hire someone new, and Rowdy would get his snowy winters.

But for now, she was kissing him and enjoying this in the here and now.

Then he moved her to the bed, eased her down, and pulled off one of her boots, massaging her sock-covered foot. That felt heavenly. He pulled off her other boot and did the same to it.

He slid off one of her socks and rubbed his warm hands against the sole of her foot. He did the same with the other and she was ready to reciprocate.

As soon as he released her foot, she tackled him to the bed. She wasn't a wolf for nothing. Even as a human, she had wolfish moves. She rubbed her body against his and kissed him again full on the mouth. He wrapped his arms around her and looked like he was enjoying this as much as she was.

Their hearts were beating wildly, and she smelled his pheromones calling to her, telling her she was the one for him. She pulled her mouth from his and slipped his sweater over his head so she could kiss and lick his pecs, tease his nipples with her tongue, make him groan with need. And he did, his erection pressing hard against his pants and her. She teased his erect nipples again, then moved down his body to pull off his socks, caressing his feet like he had done to her.

"You are a wolf after my own heart," he growled low.

She smiled. "You say the kindest things." But before she could begin unfastening his belt, he reached behind her and unhooked her bra.

Then with his own wolfish maneuver, he flipped her onto her back and began kissing her breasts, licking her nipples, nibbling them. He was a wolf, maybe not one of her kind yet, but he had the heart of a wolf.

He moved off her and pulled down her pants and she unfastened his belt and stripped him of his pants.

Nice muscular legs, perfect for running as a wolf. And she hoped he could run as one with her tonight. Her wet panties went the way of the rest of their clothes.

And then she pulled off his black boxer briefs and released his rigid erection. She smiled with appreciation. He didn't disappoint.

He kissed her belly and swept his hand down to her feminine nubbin and began to stroke. And she was in heaven. His mouth was on hers, kissing, his fingers working magic on her, and she was running her hands over his well-toned muscles, breathing in his tantalizing, musky sex.

Every stroke pushed her closer to the edge and she felt the end coming, needing to hold on, wanting to let go, and then she

cried out, freefalling, wanting to take him with her. She shat-
tered, the orgasm rippling through her and she felt like she'd
reached the outer edges of the world. Now she wanted to do the
same for him.

"Join me," she huskily said.

"All the way?" He looked surprised.

She cast him a wicked smile. "You're only a human. So yes."

He smiled, probably the only time he was glad he wasn't a
wolf shifter like her. And then he pushed her legs apart and
pressed his cock between her feminine lips and pushed as deep
as he could. He began thrusting and he felt divine.

He was enormous, filling her to the max, a perfect wolf, as
soon as she turned him. His eyes were dark and filled with lust,
his muscles working hard, fascinating her. She loved running
her hand over all those hard muscles and then he climaxed with
a burst of energy. "Holy, hell."

She smiled. "Move."

He pulled out of her and laid on his back, holding her hand,
smiling at her. "I guess you want to return home."

"Not yet." She shifted and then he was holding onto her wolf
paw and released her, his mouth agape. He seemed to admire
her as a wolf—beige and white fur on her chest and face and a
distinctive black mask on her face, the tip of her tail looked to
have been dipped in black ink.

Then she bit him on the shoulder without warning. He'd
asked for it. Asked everyone for it. Her Christmas present
to him.

8

Rowdy couldn't believe that Justine wanted to make love to him all the way. She was one hell of a she-wolf, and he could easily fall in love with her. He hadn't expected her to turn all wolf on him and bite him though. But he was thrilled. While she was still in her wolf coat, he hugged her. "I can't thank you enough."

She shifted out of her wolf coat, and he was hugging her as a human again.

"I changed my mind about waiting. I hope you're all right with it."

"Yeah, thank you."

She got out of bed, and he thought she was going to dress and return home when he had really hoped she would stay the night. "Do you have a first aid kit?" she asked.

"In the bathroom."

She headed in there while he watched her move—beautiful, toned, sexy. Then she returned and he couldn't help but take in her appearance—her beautiful breasts, dark nipples, thatch of dark curly hair between her legs, her silky skin.

Then she was on the bed kneeling before him, cleaning up the bite wound and bandaging it.

"Will you stay with me tonight?" He kissed her cheek.

"You bet. If you shift into a wolf, I want to know about it. I want to see what you look like as a wolf and take you for a run on the wild side."

He smiled. "That sounds good to me." He was thrilled she would stay with him.

After setting the first aid kit on the nightstand, she joined him in bed. He pulled the covers over them and they snuggled together.

His shoulder throbbed where she had bitten him, but he was glad that she had done the deed and they'd made love and she was staying the night. He wanted to keep her with him always.

He had a restless night between the bite wound aching during the night and trying to stay awake so when he turned into a wolf, he could run with her. He didn't want to miss a moment of being a newly turned wolf. Not to mention he loved cuddling with her all night long. But he finally fell asleep and woke to hear her making coffee in the kitchen.

His bite mark was healing, but not as fast as he thought it would. He took a shower, threw on some fresh clothes, and joined her. She pulled him into her arms and kissed him, and he was glad she hadn't changed her mind about him and kissed her back.

"I tried to stay awake until I shifted into a wolf, and we could run together."

She sighed and pulled away from him to make them breakfast. "Eggs, bacon?"

"Yeah, toast?" He pulled out the bread.

"Sure. I'm afraid you weren't turned."

"What?"

"Can you smell anything?"

"The coffee, sure."

"You could smell it as a human. Can you smell me? The wolf? You don't smell like a wolf."

"Oh." He couldn't help but be disappointed.

"Don't worry. I'm not giving up on you. And you shouldn't either." She gave him another hug and kiss.

He hugged and kissed her back. "I won't." But he wondered if one wolf's bite wouldn't work on him, would he need a different wolf to bite him? He didn't want any other wolf to bite him, and he realized she was like his very first wolf love. No other wolf would do.

Once they had eaten breakfast, they dropped by her place so she could shower and dress in clean clothes. Then they went to the clinic to talk to the injured wolves again, but the wolves wouldn't give them any more answers.

Both men looked just as mutinous, scowling faces, furious that they were still confined to the beds, though they were looking better, but they were still taking antibiotics for their wounds.

Rowdy frowned. "Fine. We'll learn the truth before long." At least he hoped so. Then he got a call from the pack leader in charge of a pack out of Seattle.

"I kicked them out of my pack for causing trouble at pubs in the past," the wolf said.

That meant the pack leader left it up to others to take care of the troublemakers. Rowdy shook his head.

"I'm not surprised they would cause more difficulty after leaving here," their former pack leader said.

"Do they have any family?" Rowdy asked, eyeing Roger and Fenwick.

"No. Maybe incarcerating them will do them some good. Give them a wakeup call."

"Or not. They could just cause even more difficulties for the rest of the shifter kind."

"What have they done now?"

"They fought with a jaguar who got the best of them." At least Rowdy figured that since the jaguar was able to leave the scene. "Thanks for getting back to us." Though he couldn't help but be irritated with the pack leader for foisting these men off on the rest of the world without straightening them out first. They ended the call then. "Their pack is in Seattle and they're nothing but trouble. Their pack leader kicked them out of the pack, and he's wiped his hands of them," Rowdy said to Justine in front of the men.

The injured men smiled a little as if it meant they were off the hook since they no longer belonged to a pack.

"Since their former pack leader doesn't want to claim responsibility for them, I'm going to call Martin and have him send someone to escort them down to the confinement facility in Houston," Justine said.

"Hell," Roger said, "You can't do that."

"I think that's the best way to handle this before they get into real trouble with the civilian police. It will take Martin a while to make the arrangements. If we learn the jaguar was at fault, we can let Martin know that. Since the wolves caused trouble at the bear shifter pub, their actions make me think they're the cause of all the problems with the jaguar shifter," Rowdy said.

"You're saying we're guilty when you haven't proven a thing? And hell"—Fenwick motioned to Rowdy—"he's a human and no one's eliminated him for knowing what we are?"

Ignoring Fenwick, Justine called Martin and she and Rowdy left their room.

"Hey! You can't do this to us," Fenwick shouted.

Rowdy caught hold of the surgeon and said, "We're getting

hold of the director of our branch and we'll have the men transported out of here soon."

"Did you learn who was responsible?" Doc asked.

"So far all the witnesses we've had in the case have said the two wolves were out of control. We still need to find the jaguar, but the wolves have buried themselves on this one. Even their pack leader kicked them out of his pack," Rowdy said.

"Sounds like the pack leader dropped the ball on that one."

"I agree." Rowdy might not be a wolf, but he knew what it took to be one of their kind.

"Thanks for making arrangements to take these two off my hands. They're obnoxious with the nursing staff too. Not with me though. I just knock them out if they are."

Rowdy smiled. Then he and Justine returned to the office.

"Martin said he's hiring a couple of the bachelor bear shifters living in Ely to transport the men to Houston. They don't have anything better to do and they're looking forward to the trip down there. Some of the shifters in the organization down there will host them for the holidays." Justine started a pot of coffee in the breakroom of their offices.

"That's great. I was afraid Martin would want me to transport the men."

"No way. He asked if you wanted to do it, in case you weren't happy working with me, but I told him you've got other plans."

Rowdy sighed. "I hope that means you're going to bite me again."

"You know, I never expected a guy I just met to want to be bitten so badly."

"You will have my undying devotion."

She smiled. "Now I like that."

JUSTINE HAD NEVER MET a human like Rowdy. He was so good with the boys—probably because he'd been up to the same kind of mischief when he was a teen so he understood them. He'd made fast friends with the bear shifter community, which helped when it came to soliciting their assistance. She had initially thought Martin might be exaggerating that everyone enjoyed being around Rowdy, but everyone he'd met so far— including her parents—genuinely liked him. Even the Arctic wolf pack members seemed to be thrilled they could see him. And she more than cared for him already. Even her pheromones were letting him know she was interested in him for more than just friendship, and his were reacting the same way—though as a human, he couldn't tell.

Last night when they had made love, it had been the best she'd ever had. He was extraordinary. But she couldn't believe she hadn't been able to turn him. So much for giving him an early Christmas present. After the party tonight with the white wolves, she would try again.

In the meantime, they weren't getting any calls and she said, "Let's go to my house. It's time to make some Christmas cookies."

He chuckled. "I love working with you."

9

T hat night at the Arctic wolf party, everyone greeted Justine and Rowdy, making him feel just as welcome as everyone else there. Not that there weren't a few curious stares and he thought they might have wondered if he and Justine had something going on between them. But everyone was very welcoming, and he really appreciated that. Owen and Candice gave him big hugs and even Justine's parents did too.

"Just so everyone knows," Rowdy announced, "I'm still interested in being turned. It would be the best Christmas present ever." He figured he wouldn't have this perfect opportunity to tell the pack while a whole gathering of wolves was in one place again in case Justine's bite didn't take. The notion plagued him that he was immune to shifters' bites.

"You do realize how difficult it can be if you are turned and can't control the shift on airplanes, while driving a vehicle, or just being out and about in public?" Faith asked. "Right now, you can conduct all your investigations any time of the month."

If anyone knew the trouble new shifters would have, the Arctic wolves had had their share of it.

"And during the new moon phase, you won't be able to shift," David said. "So if you have a wolf girlfriend, she might not like it. That is if she's a royal and has no issues with shifting."

"Which brings up another point," Cameron said. "If you mate with a royal, your offspring will have issues like you do and not have the wolf lineage that the royals have that keeps them from having trouble with shifting."

"And multiple births run in shifter families." Faith smiled.

"I've considered all these things." Though Rowdy hadn't thought of a royal not being interested in him because his human roots would dilute the wolf lineage. He figured Justine and her family were royals since she'd never once mentioned having trouble shifting. Nor had he really thought of having a bunch of kids all at once. He was ready for kids, enjoyed them, but he was thinking more of learning how to be a parent slowly —one child at a time. "But even during the new moon phase, I'd have your enhanced senses. And let's face it. The wolf always gets the woman."

Everyone laughed.

"There's something magical about that. And night vision. I could have been looking for clues in the case we're now looking into before dawn and last night even. " Rowdy was so hoping that if Justine's bite didn't produce results, someone in this group of wolves would take him up on it. Several cast glances in Justine's direction. She only smiled. He was glad she hadn't seemed perturbed that he would solicit other wolves to bite him when she planned to later tonight.

Finally, after playing a number of Christmas games, including the Santa Limbo where everyone had to wear a pillow under their shirt who took a turn, Christmas charades, Christmas carol Pictionary, drank assorted Christmas drinks and ate lots of food from chicken wings to barbecued beef, potato salad and a number of pies and Christmas cookies, the wolves began to take off to their homes to strip out of their clothes, shift, and run as a pack through the woods along the lake. Her parents had already taken off into the woods and several other families were joining them.

Some were still hanging around the beach as if they didn't want to abandon Rowdy, though he told them, "Go on. Run. I'll be fine."

To their surprise, the teen bear shifters, Kenny and Andrew, showed up and Rowdy thought they might have some more information about the jaguar-wolf fight.

"We heard about the party. We can join you, can't we?" Andrew asked. "It's not just for wolves and one human, is it?"

"You can eat, drink, and come running with us," Cameron said, and then he and Faith and their three kids went to their home to change.

The boys hurriedly scarfed down a couple of barbecued beef sandwiches apiece. Then Andrew looked thoughtfully at Rowdy. "You know *we* could turn you."

"Yeah. Dad might get mad at us, but it's for a good cause. You help shifters," Kenny said.

"He wants to be a wolf," Justine said.

The teens eyed Justine and then Andrew said, "So turn him. You don't have to mate him. You're partners. He can stay here and work with you and that would be a good thing, right?"

"Except when he can't control his shifting," Kenny said. "See, with being a bear, there are no worries."

The bears ate some slices of wild berry pie and then stripped, shifted, and took off after the wolves.

"You don't have to stay on my account," Rowdy told Justine. He poured himself another eggnog. "Go. Enjoy your run."

Justine made herself another eggnog too. "You seriously still want to be a wolf?"

"Yeah. I know there's no going back on it once I'm turned. I will keep asking wolves until someone turns me if your bite doesn't work for a second time."

Justine took a deep breath. "Okay." She started stripping out of her clothes in front of him like most wolves and jaguars did, used to doing it in front of each other of a necessity. Then she shifted into a beautiful gray wolf.

She turned her head, looking into his eyes with her green-tinged ones, studying him for a moment before she snapped at his hand with such a quick movement, he didn't have time to prepare himself mentally for the attack. He cried out, jerked back, pulling his hand free of her mouth, and then took a deep breath and smiled.

He would never get used to her biting him unless maybe he would feel differently if he was a wolf. "Thank you, Justine." He hugged the beautiful wolf and hoped her bite would take this time.

He thought she would run then, but she shifted back and began getting dressed.

"After having to be bit twice, I hope you don't regret it. Or that I won't," she said.

"I don't regret it. Go, run. I'll be fine. I know the transformation can take a while, or not, depending on the person's resistance to the change. Just enjoy yourself on a wolf run and if I can shift, I will hurry up and catch up to you."

"No. I wouldn't bite you and then leave you to your fate. I want to know if it works this time. Did you want to stay at my place tonight? We can run later in the woods there, if you finally feel the urge."

"Yeah, that would be great." He didn't feel any differently at all. He expected to feel the wound where she had bitten him begin to tingle and heal, but he was still bleeding, and it wasn't healing. She took his hand in hers and looked at it. "I'll get my first aid kit out of the car."

He was thrilled she wanted him to stay at her house tonight.

After she tenderly bandaged his hand, they sat out on the chairs on a deck with the fire still flickering in one of the fire pits.

They finished their eggnog drinks and then he asked, "Are you ready to go home?"

"Yeah, it's cold sitting out here," she said. "Do you feel any urge to shift?"

He looked at the full moon reflecting off the ice-covered lake. "No. But I'm cold too." Plus, his hand throbbed like hell. At least his shoulder was feeling better today. But he wasn't going to tell her that and make her feel bad. He had to be a wolf like her now and he'd heal in half the time that humans did.

When they dropped by his cabin to pack an overnight bag, he said, "For turning me, I will be forever grateful."

"You say that now but wait until you can't control the shifting and tell me how you feel then."

He would always be grateful to her no matter what.

After he packed his bag, they went to her place. This time, they made unconsummated love, in case he was now a wolf, or they'd be mated for life, but he was glad they could do that much and were able to sleep together again.

When she was sound asleep, he got up and took some over-the-counter pain medicine out of his bag, careful not to wake her. He felt feverish. Again, he knew the shifter genetics would quickly heal him, so he ignored the fevers and accompanying chills and the throbbing ache in his hand.

The next day when he woke, his hand didn't feel any better. He was still running a darn fever. He knew his body was fighting the infection. He wondered if he'd run as a wolf last night and hadn't remembered it. He didn't recall any dreams about it either, if he had run and thought he'd dreamed of it.

He realized Justine had left the bed already and was making

coffee and breakfast for them. He dressed and joined her. She'd made French toast and they hugged and kissed, then ate breakfast, and after he cleaned up the dishes, they headed into the office.

Not long after they arrived, Kenny and Andrew's dad and uncle came into the office. Rowdy lifted his nose and tried to smell them so he could now recognize the wolves by their scent, but he couldn't smell what they were.

"We wanted to thank the two of you for being a good influence on the boys. They told us what a great time they had running with the wolves last night after the party. They wouldn't have gone to it except they knew the two of you were going to be there."

Rowdy couldn't believe he couldn't smell them. Come to think of it, he couldn't smell that Justine was a wolf either. At least he didn't think so. And his hand *wasn't* healing up. In fact, he assumed it was infected. He was feeling just as sick today as he was last night. At least his shoulder wound was healing.

He didn't think *he* smelled like a wolf either and he still didn't feel any urges to shift. After all the warnings his old team had given him and then the wolves here had done the same, he really expected to have some trouble with this.

"If you need any help with anything, just let us know," Simon said.

"Thanks, we will," Justine said.

The men left the office and Justine came over to check on Rowdy. He didn't want her to know how rotten he was feeling because he was certain she had caused it. And it certainly wasn't working out the way he had planned.

"Are you all right, Rowdy? You look...feverish." She quickly placed her hand on his forehead, and her hand felt cold to the touch. "You are burning up. Let me see your hand."

He didn't want her to see it. "I don't think it's healing up as quickly as I thought it would with having wolf genetics."

She lifted her head and smelled his neck and frowned. "You don't smell like you're a wolf." She removed the bandage from his hand and checked the injury. "It's infected. Okay, I'm taking you to see the wolf family physician at the clinic where the surgeon took care of the wolves. He should be able to administer some antibiotics and you'll get over this soon enough, but you could be feeling poorly until that happens."

"So you didn't turn me this time either?" He couldn't help being surprised. He was certain she had turned him last night. Not that he knew about all the turned cases the world round, but he thought when someone was bitten, they were turned. Period. And being bitten twice would have guaranteed it.

"Unless you belatedly show signs of it, I'd say no. Which makes me think that you have a strong immune system that's fighting the alien invasion of wolf genes, but that means it's working doubly hard to fight an infection."

"Well, damn. Don't tell me I can't be turned. What if I'm immune to a *lupus garou's* bite?" After all the wishing that someone would help him and finally a wolf was nice enough to do it, he couldn't believe he wouldn't be turned. Not only that but he was really thinking he and Justine could be headed for a mating but not if he wasn't a wolf.

"I can bite you again," she offered. "I've never heard of anyone being bitten and not turned though."

They pulled on their coats and scarfs and climbed into her vehicle.

"Okay, yeah, I'm game."

She laughed. "For now, you need to fight off that infection and get well."

They finally reached the doctor's office and he made room in his busy schedule to work Rowdy in.

"Yes, he's human, working with me as a USF special agent,"

Justine quickly told the doctor when he came into the exam room.

"How did this happen? Did a wild dog bite you?" Dr. Carmichael asked as he checked over the wound. He was a crusty old, gray-haired man, wearing a lab coat, a gray wolf, with dark brown eyes.

"I bit him," Justine said. "He wanted to be turned."

Dr. Carmichael raised his brows. "You could do it in a more medically acceptable way." Then he frowned. "The bite didn't take effect?"

"No. He doesn't smell like a wolf. He isn't healing quickly like he should, and he doesn't have any shifting urge," Justine said.

"I'll give you a shot and you can take some antibiotics for the rest of the week," Dr. Carmichael said. "You really want to be a wolf? You know the drawbacks of being a wolf, right?"

"Yeah, Doc."

"He wants our superpowers," Justine said.

Rowdy smiled at her. She seemed to get a kick out of his saying that.

"And he would get the girl," she added.

Doc smiled. "He would, would he? I haven't had any luck...so far." He gave Rowdy the shot.

"Okay, we're out of here," Justine said.

"Wait. Do you want to try this again? My way?" Dr. Carmichael asked.

"Yeah, what did you have in mind?" Rowdy wasn't giving up on this.

"Justine will have to shift and then I can take some of her saliva and introduce it into your bloodstream."

"Okay, yeah, let's do it, if Justine doesn't mind."

Justine shook her head. "You're a glutton for punishment."

"I'll be back in a little while after checking on one of my patients," the doctor said.

"Thanks." Rowdy felt renewed hope. If he had the wolf genes, he'd heal faster, and he wouldn't have to keep telling everyone why he was working with the shifters or knew about them when he was human.

Justine began to remove her clothes. "Are you sure you don't want me to just bite you again? You already have the antibiotics for the infection, but this time hopefully, it will turn you."

Rowdy chuckled. "I'm going to try the doctor's way first. Then we can go back to you biting me if that doesn't work."

She smiled. "You *are* a glutton for punishment."

He would do just about anything to make this happen.

After they did the procedure, the doctor left, and Justine shifted and dressed. "The things I do for you."

"I know. I was supposed to be the one here to help you, but I really appreciate this."

Then they thanked the doctor again on the way out and they picked up Rowdy's prescription for more antibiotics.

"I'll drop you off at your place and you can get some rest. You can call me if your fever gets worse or if you have the urge to shift. I want to know as soon as you know."

"Are you sure that you don't need my help?"

"No. You can't be feeling well, and you'll probably be as good as new tomorrow."

He hated that he couldn't help her with the case when he had come all this way to do so. He should have waited to be asked to be turned after they caught the jaguar. But he figured no time would ever be right and he thought he could assist her better if he had all the wolves' enhanced senses.

Once she dropped him off at the cabin, she said, "I'll come by with lunch later. Chicken and potato soup."

He smiled. "I won't turn that down." He might not be feeling all that great, but she knew how to brighten his outlook in a hurry.

10

———

Justine hadn't thought she would ever want to turn a human, but she knew to an extent now how Rowdy must feel about being such an outsider among them. But once she had decided it, she was giving it her all. And she really had wanted to run with him last night when everyone else had.

She called Everett about the jaguar who owned the car, hoping he had learned something. She didn't want him calling Rowdy with the news when she hoped he would be sleeping. "Hi, this is Justine, and I was checking in with you to see if you had learned anything about the jaguar from Tomball."

"Yeah, I just got some information, and I was going to give you all a call. Mason Talbot and his buddy, Elan Powers, had gone up to your neck of the woods to meet up with a friend they went to college with. The name is Barney Browning." Everett gave her the address and phone number for Barney. "I couldn't find anything about any of them that indicated they'd been in trouble before. I don't know if Barney is a jaguar or not."

"Okay, thanks so much."

"Is Rowdy there?"

"No, he's at home, sick." She didn't want to say why—that she had made him sick when she tried to turn him. Until it was a done deal, she really didn't want to tell anybody about it—other than the doctor, of course.

"I hope it's nothing too serious. I can't imagine him not going to work no matter how he feels."

"He's just running a fever." She almost told Everett she had taken him to see the doctor and he was on antibiotics, but she stopped herself before she gave herself away.

"So how are things going between the two of you?"

"Great. He's a super nice guy like Martin said."

"Yeah, everybody likes him."

"But nobody would turn him."

"Hell, if he wanted to be a jaguar, he would have been one of us all along. But his heart is set on being a wolf and the wolves know that he'll have issues with the full moon phase. He needs to be one of us though."

"I have to agree. Even some bears offered to do the deed."

Everett laughed. "See? Believe me, if we had trouble with him, we wouldn't have hired him."

Justine sighed. "Well, just so you know, you might not be getting him back." Not that Rowdy had said he absolutely wanted to stay here with her, but if she turned him, she hoped he would.

Everett didn't say anything for a moment, processing what she was saying, she figured. "Well, if he's ready to stay up in the cold north, and I'm not surprised about that, we will wish him all the best. Oh, and though the men I investigated hadn't had any brushes with the law that I could find, I wouldn't go on your own to see them. Take Rowdy or get backup from the bears who enforce their laws, or the wolf PI group there. Any of them will be glad to assist."

"Thanks. I'll ask someone to go with me." She knew she'd

have a whole bunch of offers. But she hated to ask, and she knew Rowdy would want to go with her.

After they ended the call, she went home to make chicken soup. That was the nice thing about working in Ely at this job. She was always on call and if anyone needed to get in touch with her, they texted or called her so she didn't have to stay in the office all the time.

She pulled out the frozen chicken tenderloins and threw them in a saucepan with chicken broth. Then she began to add vegetables and seasonings. After she finished making the soup, she drove to Rowdy's cabin to see how he was doing first. And then she'd call for assistance if she felt he was too sick to go with her. She just hoped he wasn't sound asleep when she arrived.

She got out of her car and before she could knock, he was at the door. She smiled. "I guess you heard me coming."

"I did. I slept for a while, and then woke and couldn't quit thinking about the case."

"How do you feel?" She carried the soup inside the cabin, and he shut the door.

"Better."

She looked doubtfully at him.

"I do. I don't have a fever. You can check."

She put the soup down on the kitchen counter and then reached up to place her hand on his forehead. "Good. It does feel like it's gone."

"Everett called." Rowdy set some silverware out for the meal and brought them some ice water.

"Oh?" She should have known Everett would so he could check on him, probably to make sure he wasn't too sick. And maybe to make sure she didn't go on her own to check out the lead she had.

Rowdy smiled at her, waiting for her to fess-up.

"I was going to tell you Everett had a lead for us to check out, but I wanted to make sure you weren't feverish." She frowned at Rowdy. "Do you have any urge to shift?"

"No, I think I'm a hard case."

She chuckled. "It shows you have a great immune system—for being human."

"So I'm going with you."

"Yes. You are. You're not feverish. You're not getting out of work that easily."

ROWDY WAS glad Justine hadn't planned to leave him behind. But he still saw the surprise in her expression when she learned Everett had called him—mostly concerned that he was really sick because he never took off from work otherwise—and a kind of relief, like she was glad he knew about it. And he was relieved she hadn't gone straight over to Barney's house after talking to Everett.

"This is great." Rowdy had to have seconds.

She smiled. "You can't be too sick if you're eating more."

"I'm doing great. I'm ready to speak to this friend of the jaguars when you are."

"Let's go." She put the remaining chicken soup in his fridge. "You can eat it later."

But then they got a call from the surgeon at the clinic and Justine put it on speakerphone.

"I think you might want to get over here. I've just reset a jaguar's broken leg that had begun to knit together, and I had to break it again and then I sewed up his wolf-inflicted wounds. He might just be the jaguar you are looking for. The wolves were picked up an hour ago by the bear shifters who are transporting them to Houston, thankfully."

"We're on our way," Rowdy said, hoping this was the guy they were looking for.

As soon as they got into her car, Justine asked, "Did you tell Everett why you were sick?"

"No way. Not until we know if this works. Well, even then, I wouldn't tell him I ended up with an infection from your bite. Some things are just not meant to be shared." Here she was the first person to even offer to turn him and he was thrilled about it. He would never say anything negative about it. "Oh, and he hinted that I might not be returning to the Houston area."

Justine's cheeks turned a little red. "Uh, yeah, well, I told him you might not be returning. I mean, if I've turned you, you're my responsibility." She smiled at him.

"Hot damn. I think my Christmas wish came true."

"That's only if I turned you."

"No way. I'm loving the snow and working with you, no matter what happens to me as far as the wolf genetics go."

"Okay, good. We might still need to hire another shifter to work here, if the workload for our region gets to be too much. I just hope that the jaguar is the one we are looking for."

At the clinic, they hurried inside, and the receptionist directed them to one of the clinic rooms. They entered the room and saw a jaguar still in his fur coat lying on a bed, his left hind leg wearing a short cast. Rowdy was surprised, expecting to see him in his human form. He guessed the doctor was trained in taking care of veterinary cases too.

The jaguar's eyes were closed, and he appeared to be sleeping, maybe sedated like the wolves had been.

"I would have preferred treating him as a human," the doctor said, "but he must be having trouble shifting because of the pain."

Then the jaguar's nostrils twitched and so did his ears. He

suddenly lifted his head and twisted around and to everyone's surprised he jumped from the bed.

"Holy hell," Rowdy shouted as the jaguar growled and bit his arm.

"Ohmigod, no!" Justine shouted, sounding horrified.

Rowdy fell back against the wall and the doctor shouted, "No! He's with the United Shifter Force!"

The jaguar sat on his haunches, staring at Rowdy. He didn't look contrite in the least.

Justine wrapped her arms around Rowdy and her eyes were filled with tears. "He is mine."

The doctor said to the jaguar, "You, get back on the bed, damn it. And, Rowdy, you come with me, and I'll take care of the bite."

Rowdy felt his whole world cave-in with that one bite from the jaguar. The jaguar hadn't bitten that hard—not like he could have, but to turn him, Rowdy figured, just to break the skin so Rowdy wouldn't tell the rest of the world about them. He didn't want to be a jaguar. And poor Justine seemed just as desolate.

The jaguar hobbled back to the bed, leaped onto it, and laid down, sufficiently reprimanded, but it was too late. The damage had been done.

IF THE JAGUAR'S bite did what Justine's wolf bite couldn't, Rowdy would finally be a shifter, but not like her, and he couldn't be her mate. She just hoped the jaguar's genes weren't stronger than hers. She wanted to bite Rowdy again, give him more of her saliva, give her wolf a fighting chance because despite having only known him for such a brief time, she wanted him for her own.

"Should I bite him again?" Justine asked the doctor.

The doctor shook his head.

"Yeah, do it," Rowdy said.

"My way again," the doctor said. "Poor Rowdy has suffered enough bites already."

The doctor cleaned up the jaguar bite and bandaged it while Justine stripped out of her clothes and shifted. "I'll be right back," the doctor said.

"I love you, Justine. I know you can't mate me if I turn into a jaguar, but I want you to know I love you."

There wasn't any unwritten shifter law against a wolf and a jaguar mating, she realized, though she figured she could never have any kids. She was counting on them. Her parents were eager to be grandparents. It truly was a wolf condition of needing a family, a pack, to continue their species.

But she realized she'd give that up to keep Rowdy as her partner, her mate, if he even wanted to be with her if he was now a jaguar.

The doctor returned and did the transfusion again and patted Rowdy on the shoulder. "If I were your boss, I'd give you the rest of the day off."

They weren't done. They needed to speak with the jaguar, but if he wasn't shifting, they'd go to see his friend Barney.

She shifted and dressed. "We need to speak with a jaguar who knows this one. This one is Mason, even though he can't tell us so. But he was the one who left the fur behind at the scene of the fight."

"Yeah, I'm ready to learn more about this case," Rowdy said.

She admired that about him. He was always ready to do what had to be done.

"Let me know how this all turns out," Doc said.

"We will," Rowdy said. "And thanks for all your help with this."

"I would have sedated the jaguar, if I'd known he was going to bite you," Doc said.

But it was too late for that. Justine thanked him and then she and Rowdy returned to her vehicle. "If you turn into a jaguar, I'm still keeping you."

Rowdy smiled.

"I'm serious. Someone has to look after you. And we're human too."

"You want to mate me?"

"Yeah, don't you want to mate me?"

"Hell, yeah, but if I'm a jaguar—"

"No kids. We wouldn't be able to have any."

"Your parents wouldn't be happy about that, would they?"

"They'll be happy that I'm happy. If I haven't changed you, maybe the jaguar bite will. But there is another scenario. No one can change you. And I still want you."

"But you'll have to give up so much."

She smiled at him. "I won't have given up anything."

ROWDY WANTED to be with Justine, but he didn't want her to have to give up so much—mated to a human who would age so much faster than her wolf kind, or being a jaguar and not having kids. Not having a shifter to run with or play with. He couldn't ask her to give up all that, no matter how much he wanted her for his own.

They finally parked at a little white house where smoke was coming out of the chimney and a red pickup was parked out front.

"No yellow Nissan Altima," Rowdy said.

"No, it was bashed up pretty good, the boys said." Justine got out of the driver's seat and Rowdy left the car.

They walked up the driveway and didn't see any movement at the windows. Hopefully, no one suspected their arrival and the man they needed to question was still at the house. Which made Rowdy wonder what he did for a living.

Justine knocked at the door and finally a man answered it, wearing a sweater and jeans, his feet bare. "What can I do you for?"

Justine and Rowdy showed him their badges.

Rowdy wondered if the guy was a jaguar or if he was human and clueless that his college friends were jaguars. "You're Barry Browning, correct?"

"Yeah." He frowned at Rowdy. "How can you work for USF?"

So he was a shifter or he wouldn't know about the USF.

"We're trying to learn more about some friends of yours. Mason Talbot and Elan Powers. Their family said they were up here visiting with you," Justine said, ignoring Barney's question. "We met Mason at the clinic, being treated for a broken leg and wolf bites, but he's still in his jaguar form so we couldn't question him."

Barney sighed. "Okay, look. I know we should have reported this, but we weren't sure who to report it to. It's not like we could just tell the police."

"Where is Elan?" Justine asked.

Barney cleared his throat. "Elan went home. Come inside and I'll tell you what I know."

They joined Mason in the living room and took seats on the black leather couch while he sat in a recliner opposite them.

"I got a call from Mason in a panic. He said some fanatics were trying to push him off the road. He was on Bluetooth when I heard the crash. It sounded bad. I asked where they were, figuring I had to come and help my friends out. He told me the location and said the maniacs were getting out of the car, screaming obscenities at them. I told them to stay in the car and just wait for me to help. I figured if they stayed in their vehicle, they could avoid more of a confrontation.

"Mason said that Elan had been knocked unconscious in the car crash. He wasn't wearing his seatbelt and he'd hit the windshield hard. Mason was all torn up about it. So was I. We'd been friends for years. I got in my car and told him I was on my way, just don't get out of the car. But I could hear breaking glass and the men telling him to get out of the car. I thought they sounded drunk. Mason said they'd already badly injured his friend, to chill, but the men were so worked up, they wouldn't listen. I was afraid I'd be too late. I was. Mason said to me he was going with them to give Elan a chance to come to and heal up and then Mason would shift—he had no weapons on him other than his teeth. And they were wolves. Two against one and Mason told me he'd broken his leg in the accident."

"So they all went out into the woods, shifted, and fought?" Justine asked.

"Yeah. It was strictly self-defense. Mason was fighting for his life, injured, but he had one advantage—a jaguar's thicker neck and much bigger, stronger bite. He injured both of the wolves, but he held back enough that he didn't kill them. I arrived and I wanted Elan and Mason to go to the hospital, but Elan was conscious by then and said he didn't want to. When he returned home, he did go in for tests and was fine. Mason said he'd live, and he didn't want to be treated either. But he had to go in finally because we couldn't set the bone in his leg properly and we knew it was knitting back together wrong. At the time of the fight, I had checked on the wolves myself and I knew they were in bad shape, but they'd live too. I swear I didn't know what to do. I had my friends help me tow the cars and take them to a junk car dealership."

"You destroyed the evidence."

"I didn't want anyone to think Mason was the bad guy

because he had injured the wolves. He hadn't wanted to attack them. He hadn't had any choice."

"The wolves said Mason was at fault," Rowdy said, exasperated.

"The *wolves* were at fault in all this. I have their license plate number, if that will help. Hold on. I'll get it for you." Barney left the living room and retrieved his phone from the kitchen. He gave them the name of his friends who helped him and the place where they had hauled the totaled cars. "My friends are jaguars. We didn't know the USF had a branch here now. I guess you'll want to arrest me."

"No," Justine said. "We had witnesses who said they saw the accident, that the wolves were the cause of it, and we have to keep things like this from the police. In the future, if you have shifter issues—"

Rowdy gasped and Justine and Mason glanced at him to see what the matter was now.

11

S uddenly, a weird sensation was slipping through Rowdy's whole body—his blood heating as if his fever had returned, his muscles tingling and he said, "Oh, damn." He was praying if he'd been turned, he was about to shift into a wolf and not a jaguar.

"What?" Justine looked worried that he had a new revelation about the case.

"I...I think I need to shift."

Mason raised his brows. "You're..." He lifted his nose and frowned. "Human."

Rowdy began tearing off his clothes in a frenzy, and then stood naked before them. Justine's jaw dropped in surprise, maybe worried he would be a jaguar. He just stood there after that, not doing a damn thing. False alarm?

Mason chuckled. "Man, either do it or put your clothes back on."

Rowdy yanked on his boxer briefs. "I don't know what happened. One minute I was burning up, my muscles were twitching like crazy and then—you're a jaguar."

Mason's lips parted. "Uh, yeah, I've been one the whole time."

"I can smell he's a jaguar," Rowdy said, sounding like a newbie shifter, which it appeared he was, without the shifting part down pat.

Justine frowned. "I'm taking you back home and then I'll check out these other stories to get confirmation of Barney's version of what had happened. Oh, and the eyewitnesses said they didn't see anyone in the wrecked vehicles."

"Elan was lying down on the seat, so if they didn't actually peer into the vehicle, they wouldn't have seen him."

"Okay."

"I need to go with you," Rowdy said.

She arched a brow. "And do this again while interviewing folks? I think not. I warned you there would be consequences."

"Yeah, but that I would actually shift, not just strip and get naked, thinking I was going to shift."

"What do I know? I'm a royal."

"You should have been a jaguar, dude, no shifting issues ever," Barney said.

"Yeah, I've heard that one already." Then Rowdy's outlook brightened. He wouldn't have shifter issues as a jaguar? He was a wolf then? He felt the heat spreading through his body again and he was going to ignore it and pull on his shirt when everything happened so fast, he was a human in one instant and a wolf in another, wearing boxer briefs.

As serious as the discussion had been, both Barney and Justine laughed. And tears filled her eyes as she hugged him before pulling off his boxer briefs.

"We need to confirm all that you said was true," Justine said. "Come on, Rowdy." She gathered up his clothes and took them out to her car and let him into the front passenger seat. "All right, since everyone we have to see is a jaguar, I'll take you along with me. They'll realize you're a wolf, probably with shifting issues. I'll take your clothes with me in case you shift back. And if you didn't know it, you're mine."

He woofed and it sounded so strange to his ears. But he wanted to let her know in the worst way she was his and he was thrilled. As soon as she made a stop at a stop sign, he felt unsafe sitting in the care without wearing a seatbelt. He wanted to tell her not to make any sudden stops.

It wasn't long before they were at the friends' house and the jaguars confirmed everything that Barney had told them, though they kept looking at Rowdy as if they were afraid Justine had brought a wolf with her to make sure they spoke the truth.

Last, they went to the junkyard and examined the cars.

"It's as Barney told us," Justine said. "I think with Andrew and Kenny confirming that was the story before Barney even explained what had happened, that we have a clear case of the wolves being at fault, and the jaguars were victims of circumstance. Though I'll call Andrew and Kenny to confirm that they didn't actually look in the car and see the other injured jaguar in there." She called them then and asked about the wrecked vehicles. "Okay, so you didn't actually look inside the vehicles...all right. You heard the fighting and that took your attention. Thanks." She glanced at Rowdy and smiled. "No, he doesn't want to be a bear, but thanks for asking. He's a wolf right now. Is he happy about it?"

Rowdy howled. He'd never thought he could howl like that. He heard the teens on the speakerphone laughing and Justine laughed too.

"Thanks. Stay out of trouble." Then she ended the call. "All right. We're going to my place. We'll have a wolf run now, before you shift back. And then dinner. And God I'm glad I finally broke through your defenses before the jaguar did."

He was too and he was eager to run with her as a wolf.

They'd resolved their case and it was already six in the evening and the sun was setting.

When they arrived at her place, she grabbed his clothes and took them into the house, and he ran inside, worried he'd shift back before they went for a run. He was hoping he wouldn't shift on the run!

But her place was surrounded by woods, and she began to strip. "Mom and Dad and I own most of the property on this side of the lake. So we can run to our heart's content. Moose, deer, bear, cougars, coyotes, and foxes all frequent the property. And of course a few wolves. Are you ready?"

He woofed.

She cast her bra and panties aside, shifted, and led him to her wolf door at the back of the house. Then they were out and bounding through the snowy woods and he was having the time of his life. This was what he'd wanted to do in forever. Run free as a wolf. But better than that, run with a she-wolf who had finally made his dream become a reality.

He loved her for it.

He chased her tail for a while, and she turned on him, tackling him against the snowy ground and bit at his face. He instinctively bit her back in playful fun, trying to be careful about it, not knowing his own strength as a wolf.

He wasn't even sure what he looked like, and he couldn't wait to see. He hoped she was pleased by his appearance as a wolf. He was sure that, like with animals in the wild, looks had some bearing on the animals selecting their mates.

In any event, he loved how she had pinned him down and was eagerly biting him on the face and neck, his shoulder, and he was getting her back with the same enthusiasm and playfulness. Then she let him up and she listened for a moment.

He saw what she had heard—which was incredible, a deer off by the lake, and it turned to look at them, big brown eyes watching them, big ears twitching back and forth, and then it bounded through the woods.

They ran for forever, and he felt he could have gone on and on and on. He was loving this. But he also was aware of the issue with not having a lot of control over his shifting and when she turned around and headed back toward the house, he was ready. Just in case. It was amazing to be able to run so far so fast and not be winded. He loved it.

He was cutting it close though as they continued to run, and he felt his body tingling with warmth. He shot toward the house, leaving her behind. It was a fight to the finish, reach the house before he shifted and had to run the rest of the way in the snow butt naked.

She raced after him and she caught up to him, but he didn't slow down. He was putting his wolf speed to the test. A matter of life or death. Or in his case, frostbite and hypothermia.

Oh, he hadn't even realized it, but his shoulder, arm, and his hand were fine now. Well, paw. He hadn't even thought of checking it before they ran. She hadn't either. He couldn't believe he finally had the advanced healing genetics and in their line of work, he could sure use them.

He saw her house off in the distance, the sun already set, but he was dying to shift. *Do. Not. Shift!*

He couldn't control the urge and the next thing he knew, he was running through the snow in bare skin. *Cold. Cold. Cold.*

Justine ran past him because she could run so much faster as a wolf than a human could and then he saw the flakes begin to float down from the heavens above. It was magical. This day was truly magical.

She dove through the wolf door into the house. In a short while, she came running out of the house all dressed, carrying his boots, pants, and parka. She ran toward him, closing the distance until they were together. He hurried to pull on his pants, sticking his feet in his boots. While she fastened his boots, he pulled on his parka. Before he made a move to head to the house, he swept her up in his arms and swung her around, kissing her soundly on the mouth, loving her for what he had become. He would never regret this.

She laughed as she wrapped her arms around his neck. "Good, huh?"

"The best. But it would never have happened without you." Then he carried her all the rest of the way back to the house and took her inside.

He wanted to make love to her all the way, but he knew that was a no-no, not unless they were planning on being mated now that he was a wolf too. If he'd opted to be a big cat, he could have had sex with a jaguar shifter and the same rules didn't apply.

He kissed her again, letting her know just how much he trea-sured her for the way in which she'd changed him and expanded his world all in a good way. He set her down on her feet and he pulled off her parka and smiled to see her shirtless and braless.

"I was in a hurry to rescue you from the cold." She removed his parka and kissed his bare chest. He gave her a warm hug and she hugged him back.

Then she pulled away. "Let's make dinner now." She slipped her sweater over her head and slid off her boots.

He yanked off his boots too and pulled on his sweater.

"Salmon steaks, fried potatoes, and spinach?" she asked.

"That sounds great. What can I do to help?"

She took his hand in hers and ran her finger over the place where she'd bitten him and smiled. "You're perfectly healed." And she checked out the jaguar bite that was fading too.

"Yeah, the wolf genes finally really kicked in."

"Good." She led him into the kitchen. "If you want to make us some Christmas drinks, the bar is there, and the cocktail recipe book is sitting on the counter. This is a cause for celebration."

"I agree." He would be her personal bartender if she let him. And he cooked up some mean grilled dishes too. "How do Christmas margaritas sound?"

"Go for it."

He mixed all the ingredients including cranberry juice, tequila, Cointreau, fresh lime juice, and maple syrup together. "Salt on the rim or—"

"Sugar," she said, smiling.

"Okay. I'll have that too." He finished making the drinks and came into the kitchen to see how he could help her with dinner.

"You can set out the silverware, plates, and get us some glasses of water, if you don't mind."

"Yeah, I'll do that." But he handed her cocktail to her first and they clinked them together, then they both took a sip and she smiled.

"Hmm, that's good." Then she wrapped her arm around his neck and licked his sugary lips and he licked hers, their tongues teasing and tasting.

Man, he couldn't believe how much his sense of taste had perked up even. "You taste divine."

She chuckled and set her glass down on the counter and then gave him a hug and he hugged her back. "So do you." Then she pulled away and began to slice up the potatoes.

He had been so looking forward to nights spent overlooking Birch Lake, listening to the water rolling over the rocky bank, listening to the wind ruffling the tree branches. But now? He wanted to spend the evenings with Justine every night in the worst way. Not that he hadn't before, but he swore it was the wolf part of him that was craving her something fierce.

"Yes, I feel the strong pull too," she said. "Our pheromones are calling to each other. I could smell yours before, but now that you're a wolf, they're much more pronounced now. And I knew we both had the hots for each other from the very beginning."

"I knew the wolves had superpowers."

She laughed. She finally dished up their food and they sat down to eat.

JUSTINE COULDN'T BELIEVE the blasted jaguar had bitten Rowdy when here she'd been trying to turn him into a wolf shifter like her. When Rowdy had the urge to shift at Barney's house, she'd been afraid he was going to be a jaguar.

She was thankful her genetics had changed him instead. She considered what he had said earlier—that she wouldn't have to mate him even if she turned him. She was pleased he was interested in the same thing as her and that she could still have kids and her parents could love on some grandchildren someday.

He was a beautiful wolf when he was wearing his thick wolf coat—a gorgeous black saddle and mask on his face, tans and whites on his chin and chest, long legs, big bodied, a wolf to be reckoned with.

After they finished the meal, she said, "Okay, we'll tell everyone you're now a full-fledged wolf, and you're staying here and not returning to Houston, but we'll wait on a mating to see how you feel about all the changes first."

"We can. Or we can just go ahead with a mating if you're ready and want to. Once I've made up my mind to do something, I do it. And you're the only one I want to be with."

She smiled, glad he felt that way because she'd had every intention of talking him into it soonest. "Good, then we'll share the good news once it's done, and you can move in with me."

"I'm all for that. You were willing to give up so much to be with me and I couldn't love you more for it."

She sighed. "I had to turn you before my mother did—knowing already that you were the right one for me. Or any other she-wolf who knew a good deal when she saw one and wanted to claim you for her own first. And boy, I'm glad I did because if I hadn't—"

"I would have become a jaguar—courtesy of Mason's bite."

"Exactly. I love you. Come on then. Let's make this official." She was ready to mate her wolf. What if some other she-wolf was taken in by his generosity, his sexiness? She wasn't about to lose him to another single she-wolf.

He swept her up in his arms and carried her into the master bedroom, putting all those fascinating muscles to work, and this time she and he wouldn't hold back. They were making love like they did the first time, all the way, only they would both be *lupus garous* this time. And they would be mated for life.

After setting her on the floor next to the bed, he slid her sweater over her head and bared her breasts. She pulled his sweater over his head, tossing it to the floor, and then slid her hands over his biceps, and kissed his wondrous pecs. He threaded his fingers through her hair with a sensuous touch.

She wrapped her arms around his neck and began to kiss his generous mouth—so masculine, so adept at kissing her as if their lips had been created just for this—for each other, no one else.

Heat spread throughout her body, their pheromones calling out to each other, working them up into a passionate frenzy and he began pulling off her pants. No panties. He smiled.

But he wasn't wearing boxer briefs either, neither of them having had time to dress that fully when she rescued him from the cold. And all the better to getting down to business now.

She climbed into bed, and he joined her, and the kissing

began all over again. Tongues touching and sliding over each other, their kisses electrifying, demanding, needy.

His mouth took a detour and suckled on a breast, and she gasped with the intimacy she loved and hadn't even realized how much she'd needed. Then he worked on her other breast and licked and kissed the nipple, peaked and stimulated to the max.

Then he began stroking her clit, playing her. She felt wet for him, ready to take this all the way. He was stroking her lightly, harder, slowly, faster, determined to bring her to climax and she was feeling the exhilaration rising, the need mounting. Her body was screaming for release with his hot touch, and she felt herself reaching for the moon and beyond.

She arched her back, so near to the end, she couldn't stand it, wanted to beg for release, and then she was catapulted into the most heavenly of worlds. She cried out with relief and exultation, intense ripples of pleasure running rampant through her.

Their mouths melded again, kissing, tasting, and then she wrapped her arms around him. "Mate with me, my wolf."

His smoldering gaze collided with hers. "My pleasure." He moved between her legs and pushed his stiff erection between her swollen and throbbing folds, deeply embedding himself in her, pushing deeper. And then he began to thrust.

They were united as wolves, and she couldn't have been happier as he thrust harder, faster, taking her to the next level. She didn't want him to stop, needed him to keep on making love to her the whole night long.

WHEN JUSTINE CALLED Rowdy her wolf, he couldn't have been any more thrilled to hear those words.

He couldn't believe how much stronger all his senses were as a wolf while he made love to Justine. He could smell their musky sex, female, male, pheromones, all tantalizing him to take this to the end and want for more. Wolfish needs. Human needs. His wolf was saying he claimed her, she was his forever-more, and he loved that feeling of unity.

He could hear the slight changes in her breathing, hitching when he was getting closer to making her come again, angling himself inside her, feeling the tension building in her, seeing the pleasure in her expression, the light perspiration on her skin, feeling the heat of their bodies colliding.

The end was near, and he held on, sure she was about to climax again, and he wanted that to happen. But then he couldn't stop the inevitable and he climaxed, filling her with his seed, feeling as if he had gone around the world and back, sati-ated, in love and loved. And she orgasmed right after that.

"Ohmigod, you are such a hot wolf lover," she said, breath-lessly. "I love you."

"I love you." He pressed heavily against her, wanting to surround her, fill her, keep her like this always.

She wrapped her arms around him and smiled. "Stay like this the whole night through."

"Forever and ever." They were going to make the best USF special agent team ever—in and out of bed, he just knew it.

Later, they would tell everyone he had been turned, and they were mated wolves, but tonight, they were going to run as wolves again—the moon-filled night was theirs.

EPILOGUE

Rowdy couldn't have been happier for the way things had turned out. Volunteering to assist Justine at her USF branch had been an act of Christmas kindness to his fellow coworkers on his part so they wouldn't be separated from their families. He never thought he would receive the best Christmas present ever—a wolf way of life, a mate he adored, a family—her parents couldn't have been happier for him to join them—and lots of shifter friends who were just as glad as he was that he was now one of them.

Even his coworkers from Houston were coming up here for New Year's Eve to celebrate with him and Justine, the Arctic wolf pack that they'd had a connection with ever since bringing home Cameron and Faith's little lost boy, and the other shifters in the community.

He and Justine had done some last-minute Christmas shopping for each other and her parents and that's when he learned the day her parents were buying gifts when he saved the teen bear in the lake, they had been buying the presents for him—as if they knew he was going to be part of the family.

He hadn't had a family in so long that he couldn't have asked for a better one.

Rowdy snuggled with Justine on the couch in front of a fire before they headed over to her parents' place for Christmas Eve dinner when they got a call from Everett. Rowdy put the call on speakerphone.

"Hey, I was calling to tell you we just got the news about your wolf case. The men were given sixty days incarceration in the jaguar confinement facilities in Houston for causing the accident, fighting with the jaguar, and causing injuries to both of the jaguars. Elan had to have medical tests run down here because he'd been knocked unconscious in the car wreck. The wolves had to pay for Mason and Elan's medical expenses and replace Mason's car. Maybe they will have learned their lesson."

"I sure hope for everyone's sake they have. Thanks for letting us know. And Merry Christmas, Everett," Rowdy said.

"Merry Christmas and tell Martin thanks for loaning Rowdy to me," Justine said.

Everett chuckled. "He was supposed to be just a loan, but we're glad how it all worked out. Merry Christmas to you and Justine and we look forward to seeing you for New Year's. And congratulations again for becoming a wolf, Rowdy, and the mating, you two."

JUSTINE HADN'T EXPECTED to turn a human and take him for her mate, but Rowdy had opened up her world to a wonderful new friendship, to having an exquisite lover and compassionate friend. She adored him, sexy muscles and all. "It's time to go to my parents' place for dinner." She and Rowdy were hosting Christmas dinner, the first time she'd ever done so, and her parents were as delighted as she was to do it—but only because she had a mate to help her with it and Rowdy was a winner when it came to cooking and making delectable cocktails and delicious fancy cocoas.

He smiled. "How did I ever get so lucky."

"I'm the one who truly lucked out. I love you." She kissed him. "Merry Christmas Eve."

"Merry Christmas Eve, Justine. I love you right back." And he kissed her like he wanted to take her straight back to bed.

That was another reason she really loved him! He made all the right moves and was the only wolf for her.

AUTHOR BIO

USA Today bestselling and award-winning author **Terry Spear** has written over a hundred paranormal romance novels, young adult, and medieval Highland historical romances. Her first werewolf romance, *Heart of the Wolf,* was named a 2008 *Publishers Weekly*'s Best Book of the Year, and her subsequent titles have garnered high praise and hit the *USA Today* bestseller list. She has received many awards, including a PNR Top Pick, a Best Book of the Month nomination by Long and Short Reviews, and 2 Paranormal Excellence Awards for Romantic Literature (Finalist & Honorable Mention). A retired officer of the U.S. Army Reserves, Terry lives in Spring, Texas, where she is working on her next werewolf romance, shapeshifting jaguars, cougar shifters, vampires, hot Highlanders, and having fun with her young adult novels, helping with her grandkids and playing with her two long-haired havanese.

For more information, please visit www.terryspear.com, or follow her on Twitter, @TerrySpear, Facebook at https://www.facebook.com/TerrySpearParanormalRomantics.

And on her blog at: https://terryspearbooks.blog

And her Wilde & Woolley Bears, award-winning teddy bears, that have found homes all over the world: https://celticbears.wordpress.com/

ALSO BY TERRY SPEAR

Novella Prequels:

His Wild Highland #1, Vexing the Highlander #2

Winning the Highlander's Heart, The Accidental Highland Hero, Highland Rake, Taming the Wild Highlander, The Highlander, Her Highland Hero, The Viking's Highland Lass, My Highlander

Other historical romances: Lady Caroline & the Egotistical Earl, A Ghost of a Chance at Love

Heart of the Wolf Series: Heart of the Wolf, Destiny of the Wolf, To Tempt the Wolf, Legend of the White Wolf, Seduced by the Wolf, Wolf Fever, Heart of the Highland Wolf, Dreaming of the Wolf, A SEAL in Wolf's Clothing, A Howl for a Highlander, A Highland Werewolf Wedding, A SEAL Wolf Christmas, Silence of the Wolf, Hero of a Highland Wolf, A Highland Wolf Christmas, A SEAL Wolf Hunting; A Silver Wolf Christmas, A SEAL Wolf in Too Deep, Alpha Wolf Need Not Apply, Billionaire in Wolf's Clothing, Between a Rock and a Hard Place, SEAL Wolf Undercover, Dreaming of a White Wolf Christmas, Flight of the White Wolf, All's Fair in Love and Wolf, A Billionaire Wolf for Christmas, SEAL Wolf Surrender (2019), Silver Town Wolf: Home for the Holidays (2019), Wolff Brothers: You Had Me at Wolf, Night of the Billionaire Wolf, Joy to the Wolves (Red Wolf), The Wolf Wore Plaid, Jingle Bell Wolf, Best of Both Wolves, While the Wolf's Away, Christmas Wolf Surprise, Wolf Takes the Lead, Wolf on the Wild Side

SEAL Wolves: To Tempt the Wolf, A SEAL in Wolf's Clothing, A SEAL Wolf Christmas, A SEAL Wolf Hunting, A SEAL Wolf in Too Deep, SEAL Wolf Undercover, SEAL Wolf Surrender (2019)

Silver Bros Wolves: Destiny of the Wolf, Wolf Fever, Dreaming of the Wolf, Silence of the Wolf, A Silver Wolf Christmas, Alpha Wolf Need Not Apply, Between a Rock and a Hard Place, All's Fair in Love and Wolf, Silver Town Wolf: Home for the Holidays

Wolff Brothers of Silver Town Wolff Brothers: You Had Me at Wolf

Arctic Wolves: Legend of the White Wolf, Dreaming of a White Wolf Christmas, Flight of the White Wolf, While the Wolf's Away

Billionaire Wolves: Billionaire in Wolf's Clothing, A Billionaire Wolf for Christmas, Night of the Billionaire Wolf

Highland Wolves: Heart of the Highland Wolf, A Howl for a Highlander, A Highland Werewolf Wedding, Hero of a Highland Wolf, A Highland Wolf Christmas, The Wolf Wore Plaid,

Red Wolf Series: Seduced by the Wolf, Joy to the Wolves, Best of Both Wolves,

Novellas: A United Shifter Force Christmas

Heart of the Jaguar Series: Savage Hunger, Jaguar Fever, Jaguar Hunt, Jaguar Pride, A Very Jaguar Christmas, You Had Me at Jaguar

Novella: The Witch and the Jaguar

Dawn of the Jaguar

Romantic Suspense: Deadly Fortunes, In the Dead of the Night, Relative Danger, Bound by Danger

Vampire romances: Killing the Bloodlust, Deadly Liaisons, Huntress for Hire, Forbidden Love, Vampire Redemption, Primal Desire

Vampire Novellas: Vampiric Calling, The Siren's Lure, Seducing the Huntress

Other Romance: Exchanging Grooms, Marriage, Las Vegas Style

Science Fiction Romance: Galaxy Warrior

Teen/Young Adult/Fantasy Books

The World of Fae:

The Dark Fae, Book 1

The Deadly Fae, Book 2

The Winged Fae, Book 3

The Ancient Fae, Book 4

Dragon Fae, Book 5

Hawk Fae, Book 6

Phantom Fae, Book 7

Golden Fae, Book 8

Falcon Fae, Book 9

Woodland Fae, Book 10

Angel Fae, Book 11

The World of Elf:

The Shadow Elf

Darkland Elf

Blood Moon Series:

Kiss of the Vampire

The Vampire...In My Dreams

Demon Guardian Series:

The Trouble with Demons

Demon Trouble, Too

Demon Hunter

Non-Series for Now:

Ghostly Liaisons

The Beast Within

Courtly Masquerade

Deidre's Secret

The Magic of Inherian:

The Scepter of Salvation

The Mage of Monrovia

Emerald Isle of Mists